Dedicated to Lucia

In memory of that cold, wet Scottish June day in 2012 when you first saw the Grey Mare's Tail...

'Sisters are different flowers in the same garden.'

— source unknown

Preface

One cold, wet Scottish June day in 2012, my wife Yvonne and I took our two Texan granddaughters to see the magnificent Grey Mare's Tail in Dumfries and Galloway, near where we live in the Scottish Borders. One of the highest waterfalls in Scotland, it's most impressive in the rain. The determined girls braved it up the dangerous path overlooking the fall. Terrified one might fall into the watery tumult below, I began to wonder: *why the 'Grey Mare's Tail'?* A kelpie, perhaps – that dark horse spirit of Scottish folklore inhabiting rivers and lakes. What if such a spirit could lure folk into other dimensions?

And so this story was born – a story of sisterly love and determination pitted against dark forces straddling different worlds.

Some Scottish Terms

Kelpie: A supernatural Celtic water horse that haunts rivers and lochs in Scotland to lure men to their deaths, sometimes by transforming into beautiful women.

Seelie Faeries (syn. fairies): Kind fairies of Scottish folklore; good to humans, unlike their 'Unseelie' cousins.

Red Cap: A malevolent, goblin-like spirit from Border folklore. It is said to inhabit ruined castles found along the English/Scottish border. Redcaps have a habit of murdering passing travellers then dyeing their hats with the blood of their victims. They must kill regularly, for if the blood staining their hats dries, they die.

Ghillie Dhu (Gaelic *'Gille Dubh'* translates as 'dark-haired lad'): A Scottish guardian spirit of trees, shy but kind to children.

Auld Clootie: The Devil, 'Clootie' in this case meaning of the 'cloven hoof' (a cloot). Cloot also refers to a cloth, as in 'clootie dumpling'.

Bairns: Children.

Hen: A woman.

Chapter 1: The Waterfall

Fear urged her on.

Carrying the book wrapped in a torn shawl she ran, dodging startled ladies in wide crinoline dresses arm-linked to frowning men-folk in black top hats and pencil-thin trousers. Leaving behind the bright cheer of Sauchiehall Street, she continued along stinking, dark, narrow lanes that would lead her to the Cathedral Close. When her lungs began to protest, Mairi slowed, still holding the hidden book. Although she had stolen it she was no thief, for she was certain this particular book had been meant for her. The world pressed between its covers, and in those pictures and words that she could not read, was *her* world. But it wasn't the book the child-catchers wanted, it was her soul.

She'd always believed there was a world beyond the Great Whiteness, that emptiness which contained neither goodness nor badness, but she was also terrified of the Whiteness for she feared anything might happen there. Now her fear of the child-catchers even surpassed that of the Great Whiteness.

Ever since escaping from the orphanage in search of another world, she'd been hounded like a hunted animal. Now, having been tricked by a boy she'd thought of as a friend, she had to get to the Cathedral Close. Not because she'd be safe there. She'd heard that men in black cloaks lurked in the Cathedral shadows emerging to stand up on high, closer to God, and spit fear at those seated in crowded pews. When the church was empty they'd slink silently along the aisles, sniffing out any child who tried to crouch low in an empty pew or cower behind a pillar. And if they found her, Mairi-without-a-surname, they would either hang her for thieving or send her to the poorhouse. Which of these fates was worse she couldn't decide, for either way her soul would be damned.

No, not the Cathedral! She was heading for the hill beyond it where people got buried. Here, she'd been told, was a place where children could truly hide – a place called the Necropolis where she might find a secret nook in a broken tomb, open her book and try to reach the magical world of those pictures – a world beyond the blank whiteness of the very first page. Oh, if only she could read the words – those mysterious words...

After creeping past the great Cathedral, in awe of its stony silence, she started to scale the grassy slope of the Necropolis away from the path, unseen. When halfway up, she heard a sound, faraway at first, but rapidly getting louder and closer, even when she stood still; a trickle that grew to a roar then, beyond a massive monument watched over by a praying angel, she saw it: a huge cascading waterfall.

Mairi had never before seen a waterfall. Apart from rain and the dirty puddles this left behind, the only water she knew was in the slowly drifting Clyde, the city wells and taps and those places where working women washed clothes – dangerous places, for the child-catchers knew all children would, sooner or later, be overcome with thirst. This was so different. Open-mouthed, Mairi stared at the magical, glistening curtain of water, a cascade of droplets that sparkled like the jewels she'd once seen in a shop window, and almost alive. So it came as no great surprise when a shape showed in the water. Initially she could not make out what this was – a part of the water fighting to break free, maybe? No, it was truly alive – a creature rearing up and stronger than the mighty waterfall itself. A horse? Yes, a strange, luminous, silvery horse and – oh, so magnificent!

Clutching the book to her chest, Mairi ran to the waterfall and the magical horse who promised to bear her to the land of those pictures...

***

"Hurry up, Caitlin!" someone shouted. "Your mum and I are getting cold standing here in the rain."

Caitlin? Who's she? Mairi thought as she stood squinting at the swirl of froth at the foot of the waterfall, her eyes half-closed against the driving rain. *My mum's dead. Who was she, anyway? And my name's Mairi, not Caitlin. Why am I here? To be free again – at long last?*

Caitlin had not wanted to go that day. "We must do something together as a family for a change," her dad had insisted. "It's such a lovely day!" But when they arrived at the Grey Mare's Tail in the Scottish Borders, the sky changed to gravestone-grey. Dad became upset because the weather had turned nasty and she could not understand why they hadn't let her stay behind, curled up on the sofa, on her fifteenth birthday of all days, with her latest book which, from page one, had been a real page turner.

It was about a girl of her age in Glasgow back in the time of Queen Victoria; an orphan girl who ran away from the cruelty of an orphanage to make her own way in a harsh world. Oh boy, what could be harsher than forcing a high school bookworm to traipse the Scottish Borders hills on the worst day of the century just to see a miserable old waterfall? As for the girl in the book, Caitlin was dying to know more about her – and the mystery of who her parents really were. Mairi seemed so special.

Something happened when Caitlin stopped to look at the beige-streaked fall that thundered down from the craggy cliff above. It was as if she'd stepped into a different world: a world of water and rocks where hidden voices called out from whispering gullies, where fear lurked in every cranny and where she was no longer Caitlin but Mairi.

I have no mother or father, she thought as that man continued to shout out to someone called Caitlin. *I'm an orphan!*

She leaned forward to get a better view of the water tumbling into the liquorice-black pool below raising a fine white spray, and that's when she saw it: a shape that wavered in the spray like filigree lace held aloft by unseen fingers – the shape of a galloping horse. And when the horse turned its head and fixed her with hollowed black eye sockets she knew this was *her* horse and she must become its eyes.

"Caitlin, get away from the edge!" The voice from up above sounded almost hysterical as she smiled comfortably to herself.

I'm not Caitlin so I don't have to obey. Anyway, that horse needs me. And he's going to take me to freedom – to a magical place where I'll be a princess and no longer a homeless waif.

She sank down onto all fours, gripped the wet grass fringing the rocky edge and peered at the glistening creature. He looked truly awesome as he kicked and leapt in the water – even more powerful than the waterfall, and he was beckoning her to join him and become his eyes. She'd ride away on him beyond the roar of the cascade to the land where she belonged and would one day become queen – not that scowling, imperious Queen Victoria, but a kind and beautiful queen.

"Dad's coming, Caitlin! Stay back!"

Dad?

Caitlin peered over her shoulder and saw her father clamber down the slope towards her, half-running, half-sliding – and frantic. She clung to the grass, but it slid slowly through her fingers. It seemed as if she'd just snapped out of someone else's dream – that of a girl called Mairi, the girl in her book; a dream in which the father she loved so much had nothing to do with her.

"Dad, Dad!" she yelled, slipping.

She faced the waterfall again and saw the hovering horse.

Let the water bring you to me, he was saying without words. *I sent the rain to help you. The grass must obey the water of the rain and I am Lord of all water. Come, Mairi, come!*

Yes, I am Mairi. I know I am. Princess Mairi.

Someone screamed. Was it her or that other girl called...?

What is her name?

Suspended in space, time seemed to stand still. Then the rain bore her down, smoothly and gently, towards the silvery steed until...

She looked back.

"Dad!" the girl screamed at the familiar face peering down at her. "I'm Cait...!"

Caitlin hurtled headfirst towards the foaming maelstrom at the foot of the waterfall, a falcon without

5

wings. Her legs tried to pull her back up to her father but could only kick and stamp in the chill air; she saw his arm reach down, pawing at the void that separated them whilst the rain beat her downwards, away from him. All this in a split second; terrified, she twirled herself round till...

There he is – my horse, so close...

Soundless words drifted up to Mairi from the horse's gaping mouth, pulling her towards those hollow eyes.

Kelpie-e-e-e-e – come, my Princess, come to your Kelpie-e-e-e-e... Mair-i-i-i-i, they seemed to say.

Yes, I must come. I'm Mairi. Princess Mairi! Not that other girl!

Mairi tried to remember where she'd heard that word 'kelpie'. Had it been in a dream? A dream in which the girl from another world would sometimes join her – a world beyond the Great Whiteness that enclosed the dark, smoke-filled city.

The landing was soft, like cotton-wool. She clung to the liquid neck of the horse as he leapt into the spray and through the waterfall, but the water no longer felt wet. It had become cool silk that stroked her limbs and face as they sped deeper and deeper into the whirling white and all she wanted was to get to that magical place where she was a princess and where everyone would love her. No longer would she be an orphan.

Passing through the waterfall and on into a deep gap in the rock, the Kelpie gathered speed. Mairi should have felt frightened, for there was no light inside the mountain and no sound other than the rush of cold air, but the Kelpie had called her and she had come, come to claim her land, leaving behind the

Great Whiteness beyond the words of the book and the misery of her life in Glasgow. She would become Queen and she wanted the whole world to know.

"Princess Mairi is coming, my people!" she cried out.

Ahead, the rock turned from black to grey. A thin sliver of light showed, growing wider and wider, until the Kelpie shot from the cliff face out over a verdant forest and on to a vast, bright plain carpeted with yellow and blue flowers. She wanted him to stop so she could pick the flowers to make a crown for her hair, for surely a princess in this magnificent land would need to wear a crown, but the Kelpie sped on and on and she had no idea how to stop the creature. A jagged strip of blue mountains rimmed the horizon, all the time getting closer till the girl was able to make out a vast turreted palace perched on top of the summit of the highest peak.

"My Palace!" she called out excitedly, and she noticed for the first time her new clothes: not those tattered garments they made her wear on the other side of that waterfall but a long, silken, purple dress as might be worn by a princess.

To her dismay, they were heading not for the Palace but a gaping cave entrance nearly as dark as the hollowed-out eyes of the Kelpie. They were now going so fast she had difficulty making out anything in the bright blue and yellow blur of the landscape, but she caught sight of something large and white flying high above in the cloudless blue sky: a huge bird?

As they sped on towards the cave, Mairi closed her eyes. Once inside, the beast slowed to a trot before coming to a standstill. Then... bump! She was sitting in a wet patch on the stony floor of the cave. She opened her eyes. No Kelpie!

"Ouch!" she cried, standing up and rubbing her bottom. "Where have you gone, Kelpie?"

"Gone to seek out the silver Humming Bird, of course!" a gruff voice informed her.

Mairi swivelled. In the darkness she saw the whites of two large eyes staring up at her. She edged forwards until able to make out the hunched figure of a squat little gnome dressed in green. He had a pointy hat and a pointy grey beard and was holding, with both hands, a huge claymore sword, longer than him. The tip of the sword balanced on the ground just feet from where the girl stood and was even pointier than his hat and beard.

"Who are *you*?" ventured Mairi.

"The Keeper of the Eyes," replied the gnome. "But most folk call me Craddick."

"Keeper of the Eyes? I don't know what you're talking about!"

"Och, but you should! You must! It's why you're here!"

Mairi recalled only the nightmare in which she was a poor orphan girl who'd run away from cruel grown-ups before ending up astride the Kelpie with a strangely overwhelming desire to become the eyes of the beast. That was surely because he needed her help to regain this land where she was the Princess and would soon become Queen. She still held that book, the one with those pictures that she'd always believed spelled out her destiny.

"But where's my Kelpie?" asked Mairi. "I've got to get to the Palace. *My* Palace! He should've taken me there."

"Oh, you'll get there all right," replied Craddick.

"As his eyes. When he's found the silver Humming Bird."

Everything about Craddick was ugly. Still rubbing her bottom, Mairi gawped at his wrinkled face, his droopy, leathery ears and disproportionately large bulbous nose. His feet and hands were also bigger than they should have been – twice the size of hers although he barely came up to her shoulder. In fact, the more she looked at him the more she reckoned there wasn't a single nice thing to say about Craddick the gnome.

"I don't know anything about humming birds," said Mairi. Not strictly true, for she half-remembered being told once that humming birds are the only birds that fly like insects, although who did the telling and why she had no idea.

"You soon will," Craddick informed her. "*When you see it* – and before you dinnae see it, if you get my meaning!"

"Why are you holding that sword?" asked the girl.

"Do I have to tell you everything a thousand times, lass?" answered the gnome. "Because I'm the Keeper of the Eyes!"

"What eyes?"

"Yours!"

Mairi began to feel uneasy. Why should a hideous little gnome be the keeper of *her* eyes? Slowly an answer began to form in her head. The Kelpie hadn't brought her here to help him get the Palace back for her. He really did mean to steal her eyes. And the Humming Bird he'd gone to find was something to do with this. She had to escape – had to get to the Palace on the mountain before he did. She doubted the gnome had the strength to lift the claymore off the ground and his legs were a lot shorter than hers.

"Bet you can't lift that sword," she challenged, for it looked far too heavy for him. Craddick grinned. He had only two teeth, both crooked, one at the top and the other at the bottom, which made Mairi hate him even more. He turned, and nodded at something round and orange up against the wall of the cave. It looked like a pumpkin.

"I'll show you!" he leered. "Care to get me that pumpkin, miss?"

"No!" replied Mairi. "I'm a Princess. Princesses don't go around fetching pumpkins for gnomes!"

"Well, it's either that or your neck – whichever you prefer."

Mairi opted for the pumpkin. It was extremely heavy. She thought about throwing it at Craddick and escaping as she had from the orphanage, but she could barely keep it off the ground before dumping it in front of the gnome.

"Good thinking," he said. "If I were to cut off your head now it'd ruin your eyes and my Master would get very angry. He's not so nice when he's angry!"

The girl watched anxiously as Craddick easily raised the great Sword high above his head then sliced it down across the pumpkin with one clean sweep. The two halves of the large vegetable flopped apart exposing succulent orange flesh – and the flesh gave her an idea.

"My eyes are telling me they're hungry," she said. "It's your job to feed them if you're their keeper!"

"Erm... pumpkin?" he queried.

"Nothing better!" Mairi replied. "Helps me see in the dark."

"In the dark, ay? He'll like that. Wait..."

Craddick began to hum tunelessly to himself as he

set about cutting up one of the pumpkin halves with the sword.

Mairi took her chance. She was quick; she had to be to survive in the orphanage. Bending down, she dropped her book and picked up the other half pumpkin. Although heavy, she could at least lift it to shoulder height. When Craddick turned to see what she was up to she hit him full on his squashy nose with the cut side of the pumpkin, sending him sprawling. The claymore clattered to the ground. Mairi grabbed it with two hands and raised it above the dazed gnome. She'd seen what it did to the pumpkin, but when she caught sight of the fear in Craddick's wide eyes she couldn't carry out the act – she could not kill him. She suddenly felt sorry for the gnome and no way could she harm anyone or anything she felt sorry for. Lowering the point of the weapon to the ground, she leant forwards on the hilt.

"Okay," she agreed, "you're the Keeper of the Eyes but *I'm* now Keeper of the Sword and *I* tell *you* what to do. Right?"

Craddick glanced at the Sword. He nodded nervously.

"These are my eyes seeing you, not the Kelpie's. Got it?"

The gnome nodded again.

"Yes, miss!"

"No! You call me 'Princess'!"

"Right, Princess."

"And we're going to the Palace. Straightaway! Get up!"

Craddick struggled to his feet and dusted the dirt from his green tunic.

"What about the pumpkin, Princess? Seeing in the

dark? Your eyes..."

"Don't be stupid!" scoffed Mairi. "Even orphan girls know you can't eat raw pumpkin. Hurry! You go in front. So I can keep an eye on you. With my own eyes! And you're going to keep them that way. It's your job as Keeper of the Eyes."

Chapter 2: The Plain of Souls

Mairi followed Craddick out of the cave into the brilliant sunlight.

Dazzled at first, she had to blink a few times before she could clearly make out the stubby shape of the gnome ahead. He started to hum a pleasant tune and, without the encumbrance of the Sword, did a little skip in the air.

"That way!" the girl called out, remembering the Palace would be to their right. "Is there a path up into the mountains? One that leads to the Palace?"

"No humans go to the Palace," replied Craddick.

"Well, I'm the Princess and it's my Palace and I'm going there. So take me – unless you wish to end up like that pumpkin!"

"Pah!" grunted the gnome. "I should never have agreed to this job! Follow me!"

Mairi trailed behind Craddick as they walked beside the craggy cliff face, all the time using her eyes, her precious eyes, to check behind her, above her – everywhere – for hidden dangers. Again she saw that white thing high above them, circling. It had to be a bird but it gave her the shudders for the white reminded her of the Great Whiteness beyond the city of Glasgow where she came from. Would she ever have to go back to being a homeless orphan child in the awful world of that Queen called Victoria?

She looked down at the pretty blue and yellow flowers that dappled the plain.

"Why are there flowers instead of grass?" asked Mairi.

"They're not flowers, miss. I mean Princess."

"What are they, then?" she questioned, stooping to study the colourful carpet at her feet.

"They're souls, Princess."

Gripping the sword, Mairi knelt to take a closer look. Her heart jumped like a frog when she saw what Craddick meant. Each flower had a tiny face that gazed up into her eyes as if begging to be released. She looked away, for the pain written into those faces became unbearable once the truth had been revealed.

"Why?" she asked the gnome. "What are they doing here?"

"Call yourself our Princess and you ask questions like that?" he teased.

"I still have the Sword," she firmly reminded him.

Craddick frowned. "Because of *him*," he answered.

"The Kelpie?"

"Aye!"

"But – what's he done to them?"

"It's what they haven't done for him that counts! But with you it'll be different. He's decided you're to give him your eyes. For my Master that means the soul as well. So no need to end up trapped like those flowers. He'll merge you into him with the help of the Humming Bird and that'll be it!"

Mairi had red hair. Back in the old place, this was one reason why no one walked over her. Her blood boiled as she stood towering above Craddick. For a few seconds she feared she might burst and splatter everything nearby with little bits of her, and from the way the cowering gnome stepped backwards she realised how frightening she could appear when her temper slid up a notch or two.

"*No* one gets my eyes and *no* one steals my soul or my body! Understand, you miserable gnome?"

"Yes, but..."

"Yes, *Princess*! Remember, *I* have the sword and *I* am your mistress."

"Yes, Princess!"

"And the Kelpie is no longer your Master! Right?"

"Wrong – I... erm... I mean right!"

"So if all the people are turned into flowers, who lives in the Palace?"

"Gnomes."

"Like you?"

Craddick nodded.

"Heaven forbid! Hurry!"

"We're not that bad, you know," protested the gnome as he continued along the steep narrow path with Mairi following close behind. "In fact some of us are really quite good at gardening."

The place from where Mairi came, with its dark streets and mean-faced child-catchers, had no gardens or garden gnomes. And not even other children could be trusted there. The homeless boy whom she'd thought of as her friend and who told her about a large mansion where they left food scraps at the back gate, he too turned out to be a traitor. When he took her to the mansion, a child-catcher was lying in wait with his net. If she hadn't kicked him in the shin and punched the boy in the stomach, he'd have caught her and dragged her off to the poorhouse. The only thing she knew about the poorhouse was that children only ever came out in wooden boxes to be buried with other waifs in a paupers' grave, their bodies erased forever with quicklime.

She soon grew tired, for in the back streets of Glasgow she wasn't used to climbing hills and the Sword weighed her down, but she forced her legs to keep going. The Palace was rightfully hers. The Kelpie had tricked her. He must have known there was something very special about her eyes in this strange land of flower souls. It's why he wanted them. And with her soul as well he'd have no rivals and could perhaps reign for eternity – as Queen Mairi! But whilst she was still herself he must surely also fear her for she *was* the true heir to the throne.

Mairi struggled to remember another place – one she'd once known before crossing that bleak Great Whiteness into the darkness of the city where she became an orphan. Was this that place? The picture of the palace in the book was just like the Palace perched on the mountain above. Had she been the child princess of the king and queen of this land before its lush green meadows became carpeted blue and yellow with the souls of their loyal subjects? Was this why the book had always meant so much to her? Or was it all made up? Somehow she seemed unable to trace her mind back to beyond the orphanage and the Great Whiteness.

Beyond the next bend Mairi could see the Palace, high up on a rocky promontory. It looked magnificent. Gleaming white, a different white from that of the clouds that sometimes hung high over Glasgow, it positively glowed. Lofty towers topped with battlements and turrets rose up from each of the four corners and from one twirled a long triangular pennant bearing the image of a leaping horse.

The distant sound of running water chilled the air and reminded Mairi how thirsty she'd become after the climb.

"I need a drink, Craddick. There must be a burn nearby," she said.

"If you say so. I mean, if you're truly our Princess you should know, shouldn't you?"

"I *do* say so!" replied Mairi tetchily. The gnome was beginning to irritate her but she knew she was going to need him for whatever lay ahead. "And you must take me to it!"

From where they now stood there was a far better view of the plain below. In the distance were other hills: gentle, forest-green humps near where she must have emerged on the back of the Kelpie after they'd left the waterfall. Beyond, fringing the horizon, was a barrier of snow-peaked mountains. Coming from the city of Glasgow, she thought it odd there were no houses. Perhaps, she wondered, they'd been cleared from the plain to make room for the blue and yellow flower souls – something colourful for the Kelpie to look at when he got a pair of eyes. She shivered to think he could ever steal hers – *and* her soul. She firmly held onto the Sword, but what use would a sword be against a horse that could vanish like mist in a breeze?

They walked on as the noise of water got louder and louder till it smothered all other sounds: the irritable muttering of the gnome ahead, the crunch of his footsteps on the stony path – even her laboured breathing. Another waterfall, perhaps? Because of the water she should have known what awaited her but thirst had sucked her dry of all reason. Mairi so wanted water – water, water, water. This was all she could think about as she staggered after Craddick, dragging the huge Sword.

17

Chapter 3: The Palace

Caitlin's dad peered down at the brown-grey swirl below. Grabbing hold of a tough mountain plant, he leaned forward to get a better view of the cliff face in case his daughter might be clinging to a similar plant lower down. But there was only an angry pool of bubbling foam above which hovered a misty spray. He called back to Caitlin's mum and her sister, Rhona, on the path higher up; called to get them to phone for help, help from anyone, but the noise of the water drowned his words. Caitlin's mum scrambled down the slope to join him leaving their younger daughter alone, shivering and sobbing.

"Caitlin!" cried the girls' mother. "Caitlin, where are you?"

***

The sound of a faraway voice cut though the roar of the cascade. Mairi stopped and held one hand behind her ear to hear it better but it was already gone. All she now heard was the crash and thunder of water. She hurried on to catch up with Craddick, rounded another bend then stopped short.

The gnome stood at the edge of the path looking up at a ribbon-like waterfall streaming down the moss-covered rock face. There, only yards away, was the Kelpie, up on his hind legs, playing with the water. He sprang from the cascade and landed on the path beside Craddick.

"I sense the Keeper of the Eyes has given the girl the Sword! Is this true?"

The gnome trembled so much that Mairi feared his

hat might fall off. Ugly though he was, she felt he'd become her only friend in this fairytale land and wanted no harm to come to him.

"It wasn't his fault!" she called out. "*I* took the Sword. I'll need it to reclaim my land. And he's told me things, too. About how evil you've been turning all my people into flowers."

The Kelpie whinnied and swivelled his huge head to fix Mairi with those dark and depthless sockets. For an awful moment she imagined her own blue eyes there. A boy at the orphanage had once told her she had beautiful eyes and that because of this she should really be a princess – it's what made her begin to wonder who her true parents were.

"Yes, and now I need your eyes and your soul to see them with! But you won't require that Sword to reclaim your land, my pretty young Princess. Become my eyes and we'll see how magnificent our land is together. Quick! On my back! The Humming Bird is ready for you!"

The Kelpie, dripping water, looked solid, as solid as Craddick, and she ran at him with the Sword raised up high. The creature reared and kicked the weapon from the girl's hands.

"Ow!" she cried, clutching her bruised wrist.

"Well, what are you waiting for, you miserable little gnome? I can always replace you as Keeper of the Eyes, you know!" roared the Kelpie.

Tears welled in Mairi's eyes as she looked pleadingly at Craddick. He'd stopped trembling. He walked over to where the Sword had clattered to the ground, bent down and picked it up. Mairi could almost imagine a horse-smile of smug satisfaction on the Kelpie's face as he continued to fix her with those empty eye sockets. All seemed lost. She was doomed to serve this monstrous creature forever as his eyes and soul, but no one could have foreseen what happened next:

Craddick glanced at Mairi. There was something about the look he gave her, as if begging forgiveness for having failed his new mistress before grabbing the Sword. His expression changed and, holding the weapon, he scampered off past his previous master. The Kelpie appeared confused, turning his sightless head from Mairi to the squat figure of the running gnome and back again several times. Without apparent purpose or warning, Craddick jumped clear of the path and disappeared over the edge at the same time as that huge white thing swooped down from on high into the ravine and re-appeared with Craddick, still clutching the Sword, held in its strong claws. In a flash of white, bird and gnome were gone.

"Tell me what you saw, eyes!" commanded the Kelpie.

Mairi, the tears cold on her cheeks, felt weakened without the Sword and, for some reason, without Craddick. She now realised it was no ordinary sword and without it she became aware of the true power of the horse-creature before her. Although he obviously had senses way beyond sight that enabled him to locate things, she must now use her eyes to inform him of what he couldn't see for himself. As she climbed obediently up onto the Kelpie's back, she felt she had no right to ask why and informed him that Craddick had made off with the Sword. One thing now seemed certain: she was to become the Kelpie's eyes. The Humming Bird would see to that.

Like a leaping salmon, the beast shot up into the

waterfall, up and up and up, as Mairi clung to his sturdy neck and pressed her knees into those muscled, fluid flanks. She felt strangely safe. Why shouldn't she become his eyes? Surely that would be better than roaming the streets of Glasgow forever on the run from the child-catchers. Being the eyes of the Kelpie, the Lord and Master of this magical land, there would be no risk of her ending up as a slave in the poorhouse.

But her tears continued to stream as they rose up above the top of the fall from where a glistening tongue of water curled over a lip of dark rock down to the dancing pool in the ravine below.

***

Frantic, Caitlin's mum dialled the police, the mountain rescue and all the friends she could think of. As they waited, Mr McLeod could not keep still. He paced up and down along the rain-sodden bank, repeatedly calling out "Caitlin" until he could bear it no longer.

"I'm going down," he said to his wife.

"No," she begged, "please – just wait. They'll come soon. They'll find her. Maybe she's got hidden by a rock somewhere down there."

But it was too late. Already her husband was part-sliding, part-clambering, down the slippery slope towards a narrow ledge way below. Mrs McLeod ran back along the edge of the cliff to a gully where a small stream zigzagged into the roaring burn, and she sploshed her way down to join him. Neither noticed what was happening up above; neither saw the great white bird from whose claws hung what appeared to be a large garden gnome carrying something that sparkled in the rain, nor heard a scream from the waterfall, but when, later, on hearing a helicopter, they scrambled back to the path to wave at the pilot, they discovered that Rhona, too, had gone.

***

"You've got to rescue the Princess!" shouted the gnome dangling in the air a few feet away.

Rhona, her face wet with tears and rain, blinked; her hand trembled as she felt the three giant white talons that curved around her waist and, for a moment, she wondered whether she'd slipped and hit her head and lapsed into some sort of a nightmare. Perhaps memories from her recent past were emerging in that nightmare, like the horrid little garden gnomes in the flower beds of Mrs Kerr's place next door, or the pterodactyls from the dinosaur project she did at primary school, but nothing else was changed as it should be in a dream. Whenever she opened her eyes she was still up in the sky and the Sword-carrying gnome was there, looking oddly at her, and way below stood her parents perched on the cliff by the waterfall. She was about to ask the gnome what he meant but screamed instead; she screamed because the giant bird soared down, heading straight for the fall. Rhona prayed that by tightly closing her eyes this might make death less painful. It all went dark – like death, perhaps? Suddenly it became bright and she summoned the courage to open her eyes again to see what heaven was like.

Beautiful! A magnificent yellow and blue plain stretched to a horizon of jaggy mountains. On one of these nestled a fairytale Palace complete with towers. Could this be heaven? She looked at the gnome. He was horribly ugly, even worse than Mrs Kerr's pottery ones, so it couldn't be. There again, there were no devils with pitchforks – so not hell, either. She felt confused.

"*You'll* have to be the Sword-bearer now. Till we get to the Palace and find Princess Mairi. Can you swing a claymore? With both hands?" asked the gnome.

Rhona didn't know anything about swords. They hadn't done them at school. But why should she suddenly have to start swinging a claymore whilst they were flying through the air, dangled from the foot of a pterodactyl or large bird or whatever the thing with its huge scaly claws about her waist was?

"No," she replied. What else could she say?

"I'll teach you," offered the gnome. "It's quite easy. And the Sword is magical which makes it even easier. Mind you, the Princess is an expert. She'll soon be the *true* Keeper of the Sword again. Like I'm the Keeper of the Eyes. That's what did it, you know."

"What did what?" Rhona blinked again, but the vision of the gnome refused to go away. Likewise, the long blue dress that she now wore instead of jeans and a cagoule.

"Him telling me someone else could do my job. Never, never, never! Not in a million years!"

The huge white bird flew at aircraft speed high above the plain till it reached the gleaming Palace. After circling a few times it dropped like an arrow from heaven before slowing down and carefully depositing the girl and the gnome on the top of one of the four towers. Rhona managed to catch a glimpse of its head cocked sideways, looking inquisitively at her, before the magnificent creature spread its vast wings again and sprang from the Palace.

A bird of sorts, it was unlike anything Rhona had seen before. With feathers as white as snow and a beak of gold, it was the bird's eye that had caused the girl's mouth to open in astonishment: gentler even than if all the kindness in the whole world was contained therein and it seemed to be seeking out the goodness in her. There was also something there that reminded her of her elder sister.

Rhona and Caitlin were so very different there was barely any rivalry between them. The two girls fitted together perfectly. Caitlin, forever headstrong and determined, was the one who always got into trouble. Rhona would stand up for her sister, explaining how the elder girl meant well for, although strong-willed, Caitlin was surely the kindest person in the universe.

"If Caitlin's grounded then I'm grounded too!" Rhona would stubbornly insist if her pleadings fell on deaf ears.

At school, Rhona spread the word that Caitlin had read every book ever written, that she had re-written those in which she felt sorry for the characters and that she would one day get these published. Rhona only read if she had to, but she loved to paint pictures. She always won in art competitions and Caitlin told everyone her little sister was a genius. And so the two girls would help each other, never squabbling apart from when Caitlin went off to France on a school trip three months back.

Although the elder girl phoned home every day, for the first time Rhona felt cross with her sister, angered that she was left behind. It showed when Caitlin got home and chattered non-stop about the things she'd seen. There were no real arguments, but Rhona would make passing comments such as:

"Well, if *I'd* seen all those lavender fields I'd be painting them now. Otherwise it's a waste of time going there. And those little French villages you talk about. I'd have them all around the walls."

When Caitlin disappeared over the edge of that cliff, the awful feeling of separation returned. But the worst thing of all was knowing how Caitlin would get so caught up in whatever she was doing that she'd forget all about her little sister. The thought that the other girl might be lying dead somewhere never occurred to Rhona.

***

Mairi, riding the Kelpie, now wanted only to help her new Master – to be his eyes. Why couldn't she just hand them over there and then, she wondered? What *was* all this business with the Humming Bird about? She yearned for the horse to see the beautiful blue and yellow plain with her eyes and clung to the beast as he galloped up the steep path curving round the side of the mountain towards the Palace.

She thought of the picture book of fairytales she found ten years ago at the orphanage. It was the only book there, with pages half-torn and a tattered cover that had come away from its binding. When, rarely, she was alone she'd look for the book and crouch with it under the stairs. She knew she'd get beaten if discovered but she didn't care. She loved to escape into those pictures and there was one that stood out: that of a magnificent palace where a beautiful princess was imprisoned by an evil ogre. Somehow she'd always known she really was that fairytale princess, not just a Glaswegian orphan, for they both had red hair.

So this was the very same Palace they were about to enter. She remembered every detail: the elongated windows, the huge wooden door and even the blue pennant flag flying from the conical turret of one of the towers. Remembering, she felt a slight chill, for in the book the princess seemed terrified of the ogre. The door groaned as it closed behind them and the Kelpie halted in a wide courtyard packed with gnomes who all resembled Craddick, only their little tunics were of different colours. She wished the Kelpie could see those colours with her eyes until...

She landed with a bump on the white gravel, hurting her knee. The horse with the hollowed-out eyes had vanished leaving the red-haired girl surrounded by white-bearded gnomes. They peered with curiosity. One grinned as he dangled a chain in front of Mairi's face. Nursing a bruised knee, she glowered back at him. His grin disappeared and he backed away. Moments earlier, she had been desperate to yield up her eyes and soul to the Kelpie, yet now that he was gone, leaving behind a damp patch on which she knelt, she felt anger. Who *was* the horse monster who wished to steal her eyes and had so much power over her when she was in his presence? And what did these nasty, grubby little gnomes want of her?

A large hand grabbed Mairi's shoulder from behind. She turned, looked up at the wizened face of an older gnome and jumped to her feet. No way could she allow herself to look up at a gnome! Never, ever, should a girl of her age have to look *up* at a gnome! She was fifteen, after all!

She looked down at the elderly gnome.

"What are you all staring at?" asked the girl eyeing the encircled, bearded faces with withering suspicion.

"The eyes, miss," replied the elderly gnome. "The eyes that will soon belong to our Master! I am their new Keeper. Come with me."

The gnome with the chain rattled it, showing, when his lips again stretched into a stupid grin, gravestone-shaped, yellowed teeth.

"No chains!" Mairi said to the older gnome. "Definitely no chains or – or I'll go straight back to the orphanage!"

"No chains, then," agreed the new Keeper of the Eyes. His over-enthusiastic, chain-bearing companion looked disappointed. "Don't go getting any ideas, though. We can do without Craddick, but Jadda the Jailer, no!"

"Him?" asked Mairi glancing nervously at the gnome with the chain. She'd never seen anything more unfriendly looking, not even in Glasgow. "Jailer?"

"Him! And I'm Captain Hokkit, leader of the Palace Army. Plus, thanks to you, I can add to this the burden of being Keeper of the Eyes but without the Sword."

Mairi spied a large sword hanging from the belt of his tunic.

"What's that then?" she asked, pointing.

"I said *the* Sword. Not *a* sword. Take her to the dungeons, Jadda. She's beginning to annoy me."

Being surrounded by gnomes with swords did not feel like a good time to make an escape. Besides, to where would Mairi run? The Palace doors were closed. There was a stairway beyond an archway in one corner of the courtyard but she had no idea where it led to. Jadda grabbed her with his oversized hand and pushed her along to the archway. There were steps going up and steps going down. She and Jadda went down – and down and down. It became as dark as the orphanage at night and Mairi began to wonder whether they might soon reach the earth's core. When the damp air began to stink of mould and rotten food she knew this was the centre of her new world, not the earth. A dim orange light played patterns on the wall ahead and, after another turn in the spiral staircase, she saw it: the dungeon.

Jadda unlocked the heavy door of one the dungeon cells.

This is definitely worse than the orphanage, thought Mairi, taking in the cramped, stone-lined box of a room. The floor was strewn with stinky straw and bits of stale food – a half-chewed crust, some dried orange skin and what looked like rotting cabbage leaves. Mairi cupped her nose. In one corner stood a wooden bed with a single threadbare cover and the cell was lit by a flickering torch stuck into a rusty loop on the wall. The only 'window' was a square hole in the door, fitted with iron bars. There was a rusty bucket in one corner and she guessed what that was for.

"Make yourself comfortable, Miss. Any fuss and I'll have to put this on you!" he said, playfully dangling the chain in front of her.

"Go away! I hate you!"

"That doesn't matter, as long as your eyes stay where they are till the Humming Bird gets here."

"I'm not scared of humming birds. If they fly like insects they can't be much bigger than them anyway."

"Oh, what a silly little girl you are. I cannae imagine why the Master wants *your* eyes and soul!"

He slammed the door behind him. Mairi heard the turn of a large key. Wiping away her tears, she sat on the edge of the bed and tried to think with her mind whilst she still had a soul. How would a small humming bird that flies like an insect steal her eyes and her soul? More importantly, how could she stop it?

She remembered doing the same thing in the orphanage: getting up early one morning and sitting on the edge of the hard bed to plan her escape. By now that pig-faced woman who used to beat the children and box their ears would have forgotten about her, but she'd had other equally horrible things to worry about in that city of dingy streets called Glasgow – not least, the child-catchers and the poorhouse. Perhaps the same would happen here. If she were to break free and run from the Palace would something else even more terrible be sent to hunt her down? It seemed as if the world where she should be Princess wasn't so wonderful after all. As for the book where that world began, she'd left it behind in that cave. Silently she cursed Craddick for making her drop it during the bother over a stupid sword. But her favourite picture in the book remained vivid in her mind: that of her with the boy whose father was a woodcutter...

Chapter 4: The Humming Bird

Princess?

Princesses are princesses because they don't let others boss them around. At least that's what Mairi believed. She dried her eyes and peered around her prison cell at the small bed, the dirty cup and plate in one corner and the straw on the floor and the flickering orange light that patterned the dark grey wall.

Of course!

She had to be ready for the Humming Bird, however small it might be. Climbing up onto the bed, she discovered that if she made herself really tall, on tip-toes, she could just reach the flaming torch. She anxiously bit her lower lip as she disengaged it from its rusty loop, eased it up and free till she was holding the cumbersome thing firmly with both hands. Stepping down, she walked carefully towards the door. The torch was heavy, but princesses are strong – they have to be. She would stay behind the door waiting – all day, if necessary – for no way was any stupid little humming bird going to steal the eyes and soul of Princess Mairi.

***

Rhona and the gnome stared at each other at the top of the tower, each waiting for the other to say something. The white bird was gone. From the way the gnome looked at her, the girl felt as if she must be glowing or something. Never had she thought of herself as important compared with her brilliant elder sister.

Having been lashed by wind and rain on that high

path above the Grey Mare's Tail waterfall, the stillness of the air and the warmth of the sun now caressed her with a gentleness that almost seemed to speak, telling her only she, wee Rhona McLeod, could rescue the rightful owner of this wonderful Palace. As the gnome studied her with his troubled eyes, she truly wanted to help him and whoever he'd been sent to protect.

"You!" he said finally, offering the girl the Sword. "The new Keeper of the Sword! You alone can save the Princess."

"But..." she began. "I'm only Rhona McLeod. I..."

He must have read her thoughts:

"Take it. You must! No one else can do it. You've no idea how powerful he's become. And if he gets the eyes and soul of the Princess we're all doomed. It'll spill over, for sure. By the way, I'm Craddick."

"Spill over?"

"Aye! Into your world. From the waterfall. Didn't you feel the dark power in the water as we passed through?"

"I thought – for a moment I thought I was dead."

"That power comes from the Kelpie. He must've felt you coming. Take the Sword. Quick. We have to get to the Princess before the Humming Bird does."

Rhona took the Sword from Craddick. It felt surprisingly light and she wondered whether this was because of the Sword rather than her strength. Was it trying to help her – to save the Princess?

Craddick got down onto all fours and crawled to the edge of the tower. Gripping the white stone battlement with his gross hands, he looked down.

"Gnomes all over the place in the courtyard," he announced.

"But *you're* a gnome!" observed Rhona. "How can

I trust you?"

She caressed the hilt of the claymore and as she did so the blade seemed to lift itself off the ground. Craddick looked sideways at her then edged anxiously away till he bumped against the battlement.

"You *can* trust me. I promise. Gnomes never break their promises."

"But suppose you made the same promise to him, whoever he is, if he's that powerful. Anyway, who is he?"

"The Kelpie!"

"Huh! I don't believe in mythical creatures."

"Or gnomes?"

"You're – well, you're sort of different. More fairytale than mythical."

"Look – we're not safe up here in the open. The Humming Bird might see us. Not safe down there in the courtyard either. And that little door in the turret – someone could be hiding on the other side. There's a window right below us. A bit narrow but I think a slim girl like you could slip through it."

The girl peered over the battlement. The high wall was like a sheer white cliff and the window the gnome spoke of at least twenty feet down.

How on earth...?

"That flag!"

Craddick pointed to the large triangular pennant at the top of a pole that sprouted from the conical turret, curling and unfurling in the light breeze. There were towers at each corner of the palace, each with a turret, so why had the bird chosen this one? Because of the pennant?

Moments later Craddick was shinning his way up the pole.

"Follow me, Keeper of the Sword!" he called down.

"I can't," Rhona replied. "I need two hands to hold this Sword."

"Oh – I forgot to tell you. Just tap the ruby three times."

"What ruby?" queried the girl, staring at the glistening blade.

"There's only one! In the hilt."

"Can't see..." she began, twisting the Sword round to examine the elaborately ornate hilt till something bright and red, stuck into the end of it, caught her eye. How could she not have seen the ruby before? It was enormous and a most lustrous red. Although not the same sort of red, it somehow reminded her of her sister's hair. She'd always envied Caitlin's red hair whereas Caitlin once said how she wished she had fair hair like Rhona. "Just count yourselves lucky you're both pretty," their mum had responded.

Rhona tapped the ruby three times. Immediately, the Sword shrank to the size of a pencil. She grinned at Craddick.

"How did that happen?" she asked.

"Doesn't matter," replied the gnome. "Put it in your pocket and come up here."

Rhona slipped the pencil-sword into her dress pocket, clasped the pole and ascended, gripping with her knees. Craddick reached down with his muckle (Scots for huge) hand and, grasping hers, pulled the girl up.

"The Sword again! Tap the ruby just twice. It'll become a dagger. We'll cut the flag free."

Craddick's strong fingers grabbed a handful of Rhona's dress, leaving her hands free to turn the tiny Sword into a sizeable dagger. The gnome helped her to the top of the banner and, as they slid down together, Rhona easily sliced through the tough material with the sharp weapon, separating it from the pole. Back on the stone roof of the tower, Craddick and the girl busily cut the pennant into long, tough strips which they tied end-to-end till they had a rope. Having secured this around the base of the flag-pole, they flipped it over one of the battlement crenels from where it dangled to the window below.

"I'll go first," announced Craddick. "And remember – three taps to shrink the Sword right down, two taps a dagger and one tap a claymore."

The gnome climbed over the battlement, clinging onto the makeshift rope. Rhona shrank the dagger, returned it to her pocket then gazed down from the edge of the tower as the gnome abseiled to the window. He disappeared and for a few awful moments she feared that was it – the gnome was enemy after all and would hand her over to those fearsome-looking soldier gnomes parading in the courtyard below, but Craddick's bearded face soon emerged from the window and beamed up at her.

"Hurry!" he called out. "We've been spotted."

This explained a sudden flurry of gnome activity in the courtyard. Clinging to the 'rope', Rhona eased her legs over the battlement and gingerly lowered herself to the window. Something struck the Palace wall inches from her face causing a stinging spray of stony shards. Looking down, she saw an arrow fall to the ground. Craddick's large hands took hold of her legs and pulled her safely into a small, dark room moments before another arrow hammered into the white stone wall.

"One tap and it's a Sword again," he reminded her.

"You're going to need it now."

"But I've never used a..." began Rhona.

"Doesn't matter. The Sword will know. Follow me!"

Rhona looked around the room. There was a plush four-poster bed and even in the dim light she could make out gorgeous gold and red drapery and a beautifully embroidered bed-cover. Beside the bed a lucky horse-shoe had been fixed to the wall. She could do with a bit of luck! The furnishings were fit for royalty but there was no one else there. It was as if she'd entered the room of a fairytale princess but without the princess. Did it belong to the girl she was supposed to rescue?

"Is this where..?"

"Shhh!" warned Craddick.

Rhona followed him out of the room onto a small landing. They passed under a stone arch and tip-toed along a short corridor lined with heavy oak doors till they reached a spiral staircase. When Craddick started to descend, the girl became aware of a flickering light ahead. Craddick halted and held up his hand. Rhona heard voices: gruff, gnome voices.

"The Sword," whispered Craddick. "Quick! One tap!"

Her hand shaking, Rhona fumbled in her pocket and took out the miniature Sword. She tapped the ruby once and nearly dropped the claymore that sprang from its pencil-sized double.

"You go first," suggested the gnome. "And let the Sword-maker guide your hands."

Sword-maker?

The little gnome stood flat against the wall, allowing Rhona to take the lead. Knowing her life depended on the Sword, she held it up high as she took one step at a time. The voices below got louder and the light stronger...

Chapter 5: The Dungeon

Waiting behind the prison door, Mairi tried to remember life before the orphanage in Glasgow. When she first saw the magnificent Palace from astride the Kelpie, she just knew this was her true home. But why could she not recall the detail, such as who her parents were and what had happened to them? Now it seemed as if she'd been pushed back from the edge of a wonderful dream into a nightmare every bit as bad as that grim, grey city without home or family, and yet she could not remember the truth behind the dream. Perhaps, she wondered, this was because the dream wasn't her dream after all but someone else's reality. If so, then who had stolen the truth? Auld Clootie (The Devil)? This made her angry.

And why was the Kelpie so powerful?

Thinking helped to pass the time as Mairi stood holding the torch. When the flame reduced to a red glow, she worried it might go out altogether. Her arms ached from the weight of the thing, her legs felt weary and she longed to lie down on the straw bed, however uncomfortable, and let sleep take her somewhere else. Even dreaming about the back streets of Glasgow, on the run from the child-catchers, would be better than this.

She was about to give up – by putting the torch back in its holder on the wall and stretching out on the bed – when the clunk of a heavy key stopped her. The prison door opened with a groan. The torch flame leapt up as if feasting on the rush of cool air that entered the cell. Mairi's strength returned and she waved the torch at the shaft of yellow light that cut a path into the dark space. She heard a cough, then a voice – the hateful, rasping voice of Jadda the Jailer:

"Missy, he's ready! Aren't you lucky? We can leave it up to the Humming Bird now. Soon you'll become my Master's eyes and soul!"

Mairi held the torch still. From out of the silence on the other side of the door drifted a strange, calming hum. Not the angry agitated noise of a bee or wasp, but a soothing sound that softened the girl's senses and made her want to embrace it, let it flow through her body. The hum got louder and triggered a warm tingle that travelled through every fibre and corner of the girl who believed she was a Princess. What she saw changed, too. Everything, including the yellow shaft of light and the orange flicker on the wall, now seemed warm and mellow.

Then she saw it. More like a large metallic insect than a small bird, it hovered in the yellow light looking this way and that, searching – seeking out her eyes – her soul.

***

Oddly, the Sword got less heavy as the gnome voices approached up the stairs, and there was a new light: not from the torch glow ahead but the Sword itself. It began to give off a shimmering, luminous blue.

"I was right!" whispered Craddick from behind the girl. "It knows!"

Rhona was about to ask 'knows what?' when the first gnome appeared from round the corner. On seeing Rhona and the Sword, the gnome's revolting face contorted with horror for this was clearly not what he expected. The Sword swung down in a broad, blue arc, slicing through the gnome's own sword as if this were made from wood. The gnome turned, tripped and fell against a companion who was following him. Both tumbled into other gnomes behind them. Swords and fearsome double-headed axes clattered to the stone steps and Rhona, holding aloft the gleaming blue claymore, clambered over a sprawling heap of terrified, groaning gnomes, trampling on large hands and squidgy noses as she hurried down the winding staircase. She sensed the weapon urging her forwards whilst Craddick, like a faithful dog, followed close at her heels. The magnificent Sword shone ever more strongly as they descended turn after turn until she began to feel dizzy. But the magical weapon told her to speed up and she quickened her pace. The Princess *had* to be saved. Who the girl was didn't matter, nor whether she, Rhona, might get killed. Only the Princess was important. They had to reach the dungeon before...

***

Perhaps it was the flame that confused the silver Humming Bird. It knew she was there, imprisoned in the dungeon, yet somehow could not seem to locate her. It darted about the cell, hovering awhile above Mairi's bed, turning its glistening head from one side to the other before slowly descending, as if lowered on an invisible thread, to study the narrow space under the bed. All the time Mairi, fighting against the lure of the bird, held the torch in front of her face. Suddenly, the girl felt a strange sensation in her toes, as though a thousand tiny teeth were nibbling at them through her shoes. She saw the Humming Bird staring at her feet. She'd been spotted. If it could do that to her toes, from a distance and through her shoes, what might it do to her eyes close up?

Mairi sensed she must not look at the Humming Bird; to do so would be like offering up her eyes. Humming birds have very long tongues, and if the little creature were to loosen her eyes by pecking around them perhaps that tongue might find its way to her soul through her eye sockets and suck this out of her. The horrid bird would then transfer her eyes and her soul to the Kelpie. Ultimately he would become *her*, body and soul, forever. She'd no longer be Mairi but the Kelpie in disguise.

"No you don't!" Mairi screamed, escaping through the open jail door after swiping at Jadda with her torch. He fell backwards in surprise and she ran on towards the staircase.

"After her!" yelled the jailer.

Mairi was fast. She had only avoided capture in Glasgow because she was fast. She held onto the torch, heavy though it was, because it was her only defence against the Humming Bird. She fled up the steps, two at a time; close behind, as if pulled along by an unseen string, followed the reed-thin whine of the metallic bird. However quickly she ascended the stairs she could not shake off that awful noise. The stairway got brighter, dimming the flame of her torch, and the hum became louder and louder. Her legs grew tired. She slowed. The hum bored into her ear-drums till she feared they would split. She heard the gruff voice of Jadda the Jailer and the jingle-jangle of his chain. Round the next turn of the stairway was the archway leading out onto the courtyard which teemed with gnomes brandishing weapons. She had two choices: to run on up the stairs and risk being overtaken by Jadda and the Humming Bird and having her eyes and her soul removed, or face a terrifying army of fierce gnomes.

***

The cold blue glow of the claymore illuminated the stairway ahead as Rhona, followed by Craddick, spiralled down towards the shouting and yelling and the clamour of battle.

Rhona had always been the fast one – the sporty one – whilst Caitlin was the nerdy one. Rhona invariably came first in track events, went to gymnastics twice a week and her swimming coach told the girl's parents she might one day make the Scottish National Team. She loved that feeling of freedom when she left others behind, and gloried in the total control she had over her body. Caitlin, only truly happy when she had a book in her hands, had the same power over words. Rhona was hopeless with words. She really envied her elder sister who could express herself so beautifully and with such ease. Rhona frequently stumbled over sentences and would sometimes get cross with herself because her mind seemed like a locked box whenever she tried to talk about things that mattered. Caitlin was the only one who truly understood her, becoming her voice if she felt out of depth in a conversation; but it was Caitlin who encouraged Rhona to run and to swim.

"You're so lucky, Rhona," she once said. "You don't have to think about finding the right word when you win at all those sporting events. You just tell your body to go and you win! Always!"

Even carrying the huge claymore, sprinting down those steps wasn't difficult for Rhona, but, unlike at school, this was no race, no game or sport that could easily be won. She was running towards a battle without knowing who she'd be fighting or why, but she had the Sword and the Sword urged her on and, although no words formed in her head, she knew she was needed by the Princess of whom Craddick spoke. But who was this Princess and why was she so important? Would *she*, Rhona, get killed without ever meeting the girl she so desperately wanted to help? One thing was certain: the Princess had to be incredibly beautiful. Perhaps, she wondered, that's what the battle ahead was about; gnomes captivated by her beauty fighting those who were jealous of the girl. Little did she know how close this was to the truth.

***

Mairi chose the gnomes for a good reason: they were already fighting one another. She ran on into the courtyard waving the torch. Immediately, there was a lull in the battle. Gnomes who'd been hacking and slashing at one another paused and stared at the girl. Some backed away as she walked slowly towards the leader of the Palace Army, Captain Hokkit. The captain held aloft a blood-smeared sword in two hands. He waved it above his head and laughed – a thin, nervous laugh.

"Why are you all fighting?" he bellowed. "See how the Princess brings herself to me. She can't wait for the Humming Bird to take her eyes and her soul for our Master, so she comes to me for help to get the blessed deed done more quickly! Where *are* Jadda and the little bird, anyhow?"

"STOP!"

Alarmed by the shout, Mairi, together with a thousand gnome heads, turned to see who had called out from the archway leading to the stairs. Instead of Jadda, she beheld a pretty, fair-haired girl in a long blue dress bearing the magical Sword that the Kelpie had kicked from her hand. Craddick stood beside the girl. The Humming Bird was nowhere to be seen.

"Who are you?" questioned Mairi as the other girl approached. Rhona gazed at her 'sister' in bewilderment.

"Caitlin? What are *you* doing here?" she asked.

"Caitlin? No, I'm Mairi. You've got it wrong. But why...?"

"You're my sister Caitlin. Don't you know me?"

Mairi paused then shook her head. She was about to say something when Captain Hokkit grabbed her arm. She swung round and swiped the torch across his face. He cried out in pain as she broke free and ran towards Rhona. Craddick, who had held back at first, leapt into action. He kicked and punched at gnomes who tried to get to her. Rhona swung her Sword in a swirling blue arc, causing Hokkit's soldiers to back off and after a shower of arrows was launched at her from above, the Sword seemed to know; it scattered them like straws in the wind. When Mairi reached her sister, Craddick stood his ground between the girls and Hokkit's army, only it was now apparent that he wasn't alone. Others had rallied round him.

Before Mairi had escaped from the dungeon and scaled the steps to the courtyard, the gnomes were already fighting amongst themselves. Many, having seen the beauty of the Princess, had, like Craddick, switched allegiance. Perhaps fed up with being bullied and intimidated by Hokkit, they'd begun to question amongst themselves whether they really wanted to be ruled by the Kelpie if he were to grow more powerful and deadly as owner of the Princess's eyes and soul. There was already a rumour going around that he might even challenge Auld Clootie himself – he of the cloven hoof. Some remembered the olden days when peaceful gnomes tended the gardens of the Palace of the King and Queen, bowing with respect should little Princess Mairi run happily along the narrow paths that curled between the flowerbeds.

A line of sturdy gnomes now separated the girls from Hokkit and his army and more crossed over to join them when Craddick picked up a fallen sword and challenged Hokkit to a fight.

"Up the steps – quick!" urged Rhona, pushing her sister onto the stairway. "No – wait – I'll go first. I'm the Keeper of the Sword. There are more gnomes up there."

Together, the girls scaled the stairs two at a time. The gnomes that Rhona had left sprawled out on the stairs had either vanished, or, scared of the Sword, had found refuge in hidden corners. Halfway up, Rhona was surprised that her older sister managed to keep up with her.

"Hey, bookworm – how come you're so fit all of a sudden?"

"Look, I don't know who you are or what you're talking about but I'm the fastest street child in Glasgow, I'll have you know. Thanks for coming to my help, though. Could have been a bit difficult down there on my own. You probably saved my life."

Rhona stopped and turned to look – to check the other girl was truly Caitlin. Caitlin all right! *Must've banged her head when she fell at the Grey Mare's Tail!* And yet she really had no idea where they both were or why.

"Oh Caitlin, I guess you'll come to your senses sooner or later."

"Senses? Look, I am *not* Caitlin! All right?"

"Well – whoever you are we've work to do. There's a Princess somewhere in this Palace and she's..."

"She's me! Princess Mairi!"

"Wait a minute..."

"*I'm* the Princess. The Kelpie killed my parents – at least I think he did – and turned all our subjects into flowers."

"Flowers? Caitlin, it's all right – just stay calm."

"Don't believe me, do you? And will you stop waving that Sword about. It makes me nervous. I thought Craddick was about to chop my head off with it before – wait, you're not really the Kelpie, are you? I mean, he's pretty magical. Maybe he can change into whoever he wants to."

Rhona lowered the Sword but kept it pointed towards her sister. She'd heard about young girls being possessed by strange spirits and didn't wish to take any chances. She noticed the Sword glowing more strongly which puzzled her.

"Don't even know what a Kelpie is. I'm not like you. I only read if I really have to. Look, we'll go on up to the top of the tower. The gnomes can only get to us one by one up there. The door's tiny. I don't think they'll want to risk anything as long as I have this Sword."

"Okay. The way that thing's glowing, you really must be the Keeper of the Sword whoever you are," said Mairi.

Together they scaled the narrow staircase, stepping over discarded gnome weaponry.

"Whoever I am? I'll stick with the name Rhona. Had enough of changing names."

"Rhona, then. And because of that glow you can

tell I'm the..."

"Shhh! I heard a noise up above."

Mairi heard it too: the clank of chains. Jadda was already on the tower. But a far more terrifying sound drifted up from the stairwell behind the girls – the high-pitched insect-whine of the Humming Bird. They were caught in a trap. Again, Mairi had to make a split second choice, this time between the jailer and the bird. She chose the jailer.

"Up the stairs as fast as you can go, Rhona! Hurry!"

They hurried up the steps, each girl amazed by the speed of the other. On reaching the small door at the very top of the stairway, Rhona squeezed through first, quickly followed by Mairi. In front of them stood the hideous gnome jailer, sturdy legs astride, dangling the chain in one hand with his sword grasped in the other.

"Princess Mairi!" he exclaimed. Rhona glanced at her sister (yes, she had to be Caitlin) in awe and confusion. "You really must learn to behave. He'll be here any minute now and if I can't deliver your eyes and soul to him straightaway – well, who knows what might happen? He might even call for Auld Clootie himself. Things could then get a lot worse for all of us."

The girls were aware of something else emerging through the door behind them; something that sounded rather like a beehive.

"Don't turn round," warned Mairi. "Don't look at it. Just kill the jailer. Or else..."

Rhona couldn't even kill a fly or a spider let alone a human-looking gnome, but the Sword seemed to take over. It lifted the girl's arms high above her head, swished down and cut Jadda's sword in two.

"Take her!" Jadda screamed at the Humming Bird

in panic, but the tiny silver creature just hung in the cool air behind Mairi, hovering and whining, perhaps also fearful of the power of the Sword. The gnome swiped at Rhona's legs with his chain.

"Ow!" she cried, buckling to the ground and dropping the claymore. It fell with a clatter. Jadda reached for the hilt but Mairi was too quick for him. She grabbed it and immediately an intense pale blue light shot from her hand to the tip of the blade.

"DO IT NOW!" Jadda commanded the bird.

Mairi froze as if in a trance. A silvery blur whirred around the older girl's head. Rhona jumped up and flapped her hands at the persistent little bird. She wrested the Sword from her silent, still sister and slashed blindly, but the Humming Bird anticipated her every movement, darting like a determined wasp around a delicious fruit. Rhona could just make out its long curved-needle beak when it hung still in front of Mairi's face. Then she noticed something in the shadow of the door, small at first, but on emerging into the light a magnificent silvery grey horse grew and grew to twice the size of any animal she'd ever seen at a Scottish Borders ride-out. It shone as the Sword had done and was both fluid and solid. The horse was beautiful but for one thing: the depthless hollowness of its empty eye sockets, darker than the blackest thing Rhona could think of. Seeing the Kelpie, she understood the peril her sister was in. Whether it was the Sword that forced her to jump or fear of something worse than death, she never worked out; after grabbing Mairi by the hand, she ran to a crenel between two battlement merlons and, still holding onto her stuporous sister, leapt into the air.

Chapter 6: The White Boobrie

In the far north of Scotland are tales of giant birds that once ruled the sky over the remotest glens; birds ten times larger than golden eagles, so cruel and vicious that the mere mention of the word 'boobrie' still sends shivers down the spines of locals. With a wingspan exceeding that of most modern light aircraft, they had enormous hooked beaks that could swallow cows whole, let alone people. They were superb swimmers owing to webbed feet larger than boat paddles, and these were armed with talons that made those of an eagle look like toothpicks.

Each boobrie was an army in miniature, but the most fearsome thing about this creature was its nature: vicious is far too gentle a word. The boobries of old took enormous pleasure in tormenting those weaker than themselves, which included most living creatures within flying distance. But one of their number was different: the White Boobrie.

Maybe we are all born with an equal opposite somewhere in the universe; a balance of nature, perhaps? Caitlin and Rhona happened to be equal and opposite *and* sisters, but both were kind and good. For the two girls their differences bonded them in a friendship that made them inseparable, but the gentle White Boobrie was offspring to the foulest boobrie ever to stalk the land; a bird that was totally black and reported to be in league with Auld Clootie.

The Black Boobrie, suspicious of the gleaming white egg that emerged one day from his wife, rolled the thing from their nest into a steep gully. The size of a large pumpkin, it tumbled from the boobrie eerie high up on the cliff face to the valley below. It should have shattered into a thousand fragments – the Black Boobrie's intention – but it didn't, for the white chick curled up inside was not only strong but possessed an extraordinary magic.

The egg was found by the Seelie Faeries. Somehow they knew it had to be very special. It took five of them to drag the egg away from the craggy mountain of the Black Boobrie into the Faerie Forest. Here, in a hollow tree, they covered it with cloths of gold weave and garlands of flowers, guarding it day and night until it hatched.

There was great excitement when a tapping sound was heard coming from inside the egg. A crowd of faeries gathered around and watched as a white beak broke free from the thick shell. The beak pecked away and the hole grew until the White Boobrie's head appeared and blinked at his rescuers. The shell split open and the boobrie chick staggered to his feet and spread his new wings.

The faeries knew from the eyes of the White Boobrie that he was the exact opposite of the Black Boobrie; something there revealed that he was as good as the father was bad. They fed and cared for the large white chick as one of their own and he grew bigger and stronger by the day. Not before long, they taught him to fly and quite soon he was able to out-perform even the most able of faeries with his aeronautics. But he was still young.

When his father saw there were no remains of the white shell at the bottom of his mountain he guessed that his son must have survived and feared the good that would emerge from that white egg as others feared his evil. He ordered all boobries in his area, plus other creatures subject to Auld Clootie, to seek out and destroy the White Boobrie. After the Seelie Faeries got wind of this, realising their magical find was yet youthful and no match against the power of the father, they led him one day to the edge of their forest before the first light of dawn and bade him farewell, urging him to fly south to the gentler hills beyond the lowlands. There, he was told, he could grow strong with their Seelie Faery brethren until old enough to use his special powers. These might one day be needed, they said, should a kelpie ever take over a nearby waterfall.

***

Both girls closed their eyes as they dropped like stones towards the raging battle below. That is, until each felt something close tenderly around her waist, whereupon they immediately shot back up high, high, high into the sky.

Rhona opened her eyes first. Way below, the Palace perched on a cliff, its inner courtyard teeming with tiny figures that from where she hung looked like painted ants. She tried to make out Craddick, to see whether he was winning the fight against Captain Hokkit, but it was impossible to work out who was who. She turned to see her sister dangling from the other clawed foot of the vast white bird.

"Caitlin?" she called out. The girl remained limp. She tried "Mairi?" The girl responded by opening her eyes and staring at her. She still held the dungeon torch, and Rhona, the Sword.

"Mairi, are you really a princess? I mean, in this world we're now in?" Mairi nodded. She looked even more terrified than Rhona felt. "What is this big white bird? We were going to die, you know, and I couldn't let that horrid silver Humming Bird poke out your eyes. If you were going to die anyway then I wanted it to be with me. With your sister."

"I don't have a sister. But yes, it's all to do with my eyes. I knew he was going to get my eyes. Whenever I feel him close I want him to have them – my soul too – but... oh Rhona – it is Rhona, isn't it?"

"Sure!"

"I'm so scared, Rhona. And I do remember the stories now. Stories from before I ended up as an orphan in Glasgow. About a great white bird, but... oh, no!"

Rhona saw why Mairi had stopped short. Below and behind them, a horse galloped in the sky; the same magnificent, eyeless horse that caused her sister to freeze on the Palace tower. The bird must have sensed the horse as well for those massive wings beat faster and the White Boobrie increased his speed, widening the gap between them and the Kelpie. The Kelpie also quickened his pace. It had become a race for the forest. As the band of green on the horizon grew, the gap between horse and boobrie seemed to shrink... until something extraordinary happened.

Rhona felt a tightening of those loving claws about her waist. She was looking anxiously at the impossibly high clouds dappling the blue firmament above when suddenly they sped upwards as if released from a catapult, and, in a great arc, curved deep down into the forest leaving the Kelpie and his little Humming Bird accomplice way behind. The giant bird slowed before landing in a cool glade. Both girls were set free onto soft grass as the White Boobrie unclasped his claws. He strutted sideways and cocked his head, fixing first

Mairi, then Rhona, with a warm, golden eye.

Some magical creatures have no need for speech and such was the case with the White Boobrie. He could converse with the girls through his eye and this was telling them to wait and to trust no one until the Seelie Faeries arrived. It also seemed to say that Rhona should, for the time being, remain the Keeper of the Sword for although the Sword had been given to the King and Queen to protect the Princess, the power of the Kelpie and his hold over the older girl were so strong that in Mairi's hands the weapon might be turned against her.

The White Boobrie left. Nearby, a murmuring burn trickled a thin course beside a line of silver birches. Mairi sizzled the torch in the water and left it there, floating and swirling. She wanted nothing that reminded her of the Palace dungeon. Then the girls, both thirsty, knelt and drank with cupped hands.

Knowing they could trust the White Boobrie, and feeling snug and safe in the forest glade, they sat side by side with their backs to a tree and waited. They began to talk: first Mairi, then Rhona.

As Mairi talked, Rhona knew this had to be her sister Caitlin from the way she used words, but the other girl spoke of such strange things: distant memories of a happy early childhood as the Princess running around in the Palace grounds, chatting to the royal garden gnomes (Rhona had to hide her smile because as far as she was concerned garden gnomes were naff ornaments kept by old ladies with neat little gardens). When her sister got onto the horrors of the orphanage in the time of Queen Victoria the girl changed; angered and upset, tears streamed from Rhona's eyes as she heard about the beatings and the lice and the cockroaches and the food barely fit for pigs. Nevertheless, she was proud to learn how her sister escaped and survived in the streets by wits alone. She even laughed on hearing that Mairi could outrun the fastest child-catcher. But this also worried her for Mairi's spitting image, Caitlin, never ran anywhere. She was a total bookworm.

Rhona amazed Mairi with details of life in twenty-first century Scotland. She talked about school, about the boys she liked and the boys she didn't ("I honestly think Caitlin should have a boyfriend now she's fifteen," she said) and about school sports, i-pads, the telly, Border ride-outs and Selena Gomez.

In the middle of singing a track from her Gomez album, Rhona went quiet. She had a strange feeling they were being watched by invisible pairs of eyes. Mairi too. They stood and peered around. The silent trees gave away nothing and shafts of sunlight that pierced the gaps in the canopy above merely dappled patterns onto the forest floor. Rhona picked up the Sword before cautiously approaching a clump of bushes at the edge of the glade – bushes that she was certain hadn't been there before they sat down. When the clump began to move towards her she gasped and stepped backwards.

"It's all right," said one of the bushes. "You can put down your Sword. See – it's not glowing! It always glows if the Princess is in danger."

"But..." began Rhona, lowering the Sword.

Another bush came forwards, transforming into a little green figure bearing diaphanous emerald-coloured wings. Immediately, all the other leafy shrubs surrounding the girls turned human and soon they were encircled by hundreds of Seelie Faeries. The one who'd addressed them raised his hand in greeting:

"Welcome to our forest. Didn't mean to startle you but we had to be sure – sure the Kelpie hadn't followed you. He must never know this place, or else who knows what might happen? Oh, you must be starving. Quick – this way. We'll have to walk because you can't fly, but first we must blindfold you."

Rhona and Mairi looked at each other. Mairi nodded and Rhona felt reassured.

"Not even the White Boobrie knows where we'll lead you to. Better that way. We can take no risks when the eyes of the Princess are at stake!"

Mairi touched her eyelids as if to make sure her eyes were still there. A pretty little girl faery, with hair the colour of corn caught by early morning sun, smiled and held up two delicate bands of golden silk.

"Please don't be afraid," she said. "Here – the Princess first."

Mairi frowned slightly as the faery girl reached up with one of the silken bands and tenderly wrapped it around her face to cover her eyes. She did the same for Rhona.

"I'm Fiona – Fiona of the Bell-Flooer. The one who scared you and spoke first is my father. We all call him Muckle Lugs ('Big Ears') because of his ears!"

Muckle Lugs chuckled.

"Enough of that, Fiona! You and the others take the two girls home, give them rest and feed them. They must be starving."

Suddenly, Rhona realised how hungry she was. At the Grey Mare's Tail she'd had no chance to eat her picnic what with the wind and the rain and then Caitlin disappearing.

They seemed to walk forever. Rhona should have

felt frightened being led along a path strewn with rocks and criss-crossed by tree roots whilst branches and creepers continually brushed her arms and legs, but instead of feeling fear she was filled with a strange happiness. With the Sword in one hand and the other held by one of the faeries, she'd banished all dark thoughts. Her mind was aglow with confidence and with pride for her 'sister'. No words were spoken between them, but here, in the company of the faery people, there seemed to be no need for words; only for trust and love. And whether or not Mairi was truly Caitlin, there was something very special between them.

They came to a halt beside the sound of flowing water. Rhona's band was removed. She and Mairi were standing at the doorway of a small wooden house roofed by matted reeds. It was one of many, so well-camouflaged amongst the trees it seemed as if they had grown like toadstools from the forest floor. Eager faery faces peered at both girls as they took in their surroundings.

"Haven't I been here before?" asked Mairi.

"You remember? Why, of course – when you were a child! Many times. You often came here to play with me and my little friends." A chorus of girly giggles warmed Mairi's spirit. "That was before *he* came and destroyed your land – before we were forced to hide ourselves from evil forces and before he began to wipe out your memory, waiting for when he could get hold of the Humming Bird and for your coming of age. It was the White Boobrie who rescued you in time and took you to another world. A world whose harshness he thought might also give you the strength to one day face the Kalpie. That day has come, Mairi. You're strong, though still weak compared with him. That's why..."

Fiona turned to Rhona.

"Are you the true Keeper of the Sword? The Sword's the one thing the Kelpie fears above everything else. Some say only the Sword might destroy the Humming Bird. Strange how it was brought to us by the White Boobrie yet in *his* claws has no power to destroy that evil. It's got to be the true Keeper of the Sword, Rhona. Does it not glow in your hands when the Princess is in danger?"

"Aye! Blue," affirmed Rhona.

"Blue?" Fiona frowned, puzzled.

Rhona looked anxiously at the Sword. The confidence she'd felt walking along that forest trail faded like the early morning mist that sometimes hovered above the River Tweed when she crossed the bridge to the bus stop in Melrose on her way to Earlston High School. She was into sport right enough, but had no fencing skills and anything to do with fighting was abhorrent to her.

"No, you won't let the Princess down. I'm sure of it," insisted Fiona as if reading the other girl's mind. "But enough of my patter! Come inside. Make yourselves comfortable whilst my friends prepare a meal."

Fiona came up to the girls' elbows, and they had to stoop low to avoid bumping their heads on the beam supporting the roof. They expected they'd have to crawl around like animals on all fours in the tiny house and were quite unprepared for what happened after crossing the threshold. Not only were they able to stand, but they appeared to be in a vast and leafy space like a magnificent natural cathedral. It was bright, not dark, and high up in the canopy above light filtering through the leaves was fragmented into myriads of coloured gems. A building, yet not a building; Rhona could think of no word to describe the place.

"I... I just..." she began.

But Mairi had already taken off in excitement towards the other end of the green and brown amphitheatre.

"I remember, I remember!" she shrieked. As she ran, a bed appeared from nowhere. Mairi threw herself across the bed and laughed and laughed. "Come here, Rhona! There'll be one for you too."

True enough, as Rhona approached her sister-look-alike, another bed with a tartan quilted cover materialized before her eyes. She sat on the edge of it, grinning at Mairi.

"Been here before, then? I guess you really are Princess Mairi and not Caitlin!"

"Rhona, this is so wonderful to be back! And yes, I *do* remember Fiona. She was one of my best friends here in the forest, only then we were much the same size."

Soon the girls were tucking into bowlfuls of delicious vegetables and fruit and drinking nectar juice, a sweet-scented drink that had a curious calming effect. In a short while they'd forgotten all about the Kelpie and the Humming Bird; even that terrifying journey dangled from the talons of the White Boobrie seemed but a distant memory. They joked, laughed and played with the faery children as if time no longer held any challenge, and the space they were in changed constantly, like a giant revolving kaleidoscope. When they finally got to bed, blissfully happy, each girl sank into a deep but disturbing sleep.

Chapter 7: The Woodcutter's Son

Mairi flitted from one world to another:

She dreamt she was in a strange place wearing strange clothes – a skirt way too short, a ribbon around her neck rather than in her hair, and polished shoes. In Glasgow, on the other side of the Necropolis, shoes were things that only other girls – girls with families – had. Now she was in a dream world of children and very few adults, but the adults were kind and friendly. She sat in a room full of teenagers like her. Rhona wasn't there and this troubled her. She wanted to be with Rhona, for here Rhona seemed very special to her. Then a horse made out of solid water entered and destroyed the peace of the room; the kids scattered and the woman hid her face as the horse approached Mairi. Although without eyes, it sensed where and who she was and she knew she must give him her eyes. That dream stopped as soon as she climbed onto the liquid back of the horse, and next thing she was a small child once more. Not in the dark streets of Glasgow, but here in the forest. A tall man in splendid clothes was with her and he smiled, for going to the forest together was their secret; no one else must know, he'd told her. They'd come to see someone special, but that wasn't why Mairi felt so excited; it was because she called the man 'Father' and he was carrying a huge Sword with a ruby lodged in its hilt.

A cockerel crowed. Mairi opened her eyes and wiped away the tears. A burst of orange sunlight illuminated the entrance. She turned and whispered to

Rhona in the bed beside her:

"Are you awake?" she asked. The other girl stirred and rolled over. Mairi got out of bed, tip-toed to the adjacent bed and shook Rhona.

"Wake up!"

Rhona sat up, blinking.

"I was dreaming so heavily," she said.

"Shhh!" cautioned Mairi. "Me too. I remember so much more after that last dream. I was with my father. Here in the forest. Quick. Outside – before the others wake up."

Rhona slipped sleepily from her bed.

"Bring the Sword," Mairi instructed. Her sister retrieved the shrunken claymore from beneath the pretty plaid bed cover. "Follow me!"

Quietly, they crept past Fiona and Muckle Lugs who were still fast asleep. The room had shrunk to the size of a small hut, but no longer did things like this surprise Rhona. She was totally resigned to being in a magical world – a strange land set in a different dimension. She followed Mairi along a path that wound its way between the faeries' green and leafy homes before disappearing into the forest.

"Look, I don't think we should be doing this," she called out. Mairi stopped and turned.

"I know what I'm doing," she replied. "It's all coming back to me now. And I recognise this place."

"We're not supposed to know. That's why they blindfolded us. This could be dangerous."

"Shhh!" Mairi held up a silencing finger to the other girl. "Just stay close behind me."

Rhona narrowed the gap between herself and her 'sister in another dimension', trailing the claymore and biting her lower lip; biting her lip was what she always did at school or home when she knew she was doing something wrong. Soon the faeries' cheerful glade was left far behind and the forest had become a dismal place lit by a cool morning light that cut through gaps between trees. Beyond a tangle of undergrowth, round which the path snaked, Rhona made out a stone wall partly covered by creepers and branches. Closer, it became clear this was a ruined tower hidden in the forest.

"Let's go back," she said. "I'm frightened. We don't know who..."

A rustle in the undergrowth silenced her. She raised the Sword which now glowed with a more ominous blue.

"Only a rabbit or something. See! I was right. It *is* along this path."

"What?"

"The tower."

Rhona looked anxiously up at the grim tower.

"That creepy place? Look at the Sword, Mairi! It's warning us."

"This is where we used to play. Me and Lachlan. Whilst our fathers talked."

"Lachlan?"

"Aye! The only place we could meet up. He was the woodcutter's son. His father worked for the laird who lived here. We played in the courtyard. It was such fun. He was my best friend, you know. I remember my father saying it was okay for a princess to play with a commoner in the forest because the forest belonged to the faeries – but I cried when he said Lachlan would never be allowed into the Palace. That last time was different, though."

"Last time?"

"Like in my dream. My daddy had the Sword – the one you're holding. He was in a hurry. Something to do with Lachlan and the White Boobrie, I'm sure of it. Oh, I wish that cockerel hadn't woken me up!"

"Don't let's go any further. The tower's too scary – all overgrown and..."

Rhona jumped in response to another rustle from the bushes. Mairi laughed when a small bunny broke cover and darted out in front of her.

"Told you!" she exclaimed. "Come on. He might be here. Don't you get it? My father was trying to tell me something in my dream. About bringing the Sword to Lachlan. He'll be – well, my age now. Fifteen. I kept a count of those cold winters in Glasgow. We shared the same birthday, see."

"My sister who looks just like you turned fifteen yesterday," announced Rhona. So..."

"Fifteen yesterday? Of course! The Palace. My father explained it once. Fifteen battlements to each tower – fifteen rooms on every floor and fifteen flower beds in the gardens. When I reach fifteen I must..." Mairi frowned, as if trying hard to recall. "Something," she said hurriedly. "I must do something when I'm fifteen. Or *be* someone. So – here goes. LACHLAN!" she shouted between open hands.

The rabbit, who'd hopped on ahead, stopped and turned to face the girls. Mairi called for Lachlan again and again. The rabbit lolloped back towards them. Each time Mairi called out, the wee animal blinked and twitched his nose meaningfully.

"Mairi..." began Rhona.

"It's no use! The place must be abandoned. They probably killed the laird together with my parents. I just thought..."

"Mairi, that rabbit! It's as if he's trying to tell you something."

Mairi looked down and beckoned to the rabbit. The creature swivelled and hopped off along the path.

"Perhaps he's knows something," suggested Rhona. "Maybe he recognised the name you called out."

"Lachlan?"

"Aye – but..."

"You stay here if you like. I'm following him."

Reluctant to be left on her own, Rhona stuck close behind the older girl. The Sword now shone with a bright blue fire that cast long shadows into the forest. Another bend and they reached the tower entrance overhung with trailing brambles. The rabbit held back, as if aware of the tower's awful secret.

"I really am scared, sis – I mean Mairi. I'm not going any further!"

"He took us here. He must know about Lachlan. Give me the Sword. I'll go in and you stay with the bunny." The rabbit nodded – unmistakably. Rhona had no choice in the matter. "Run back to Fiona and her people if I'm not out after you count to a hundred. No... make it two hundred."

The rabbit looked up at Rhona and smiled when she started to count; it smiled because its face was starting to change. Slowly and surely, after the girl had handed the Sword to Mairi, who disappeared through the dark, ruined doorway, the animal transformed into a tiny green figure even smaller than Fiona and the other Seelie Faeries.

***

Mairi regretted her decision as soon as she entered the old tower.

She struggled to remember the place as it had been when she was little, for everything was changed beyond recognition. The wide staircase to the upper floors, where her father and the laird would sit and talk, had crumbled away leaving a large hollow space. Somewhere beyond that space was the courtyard where two young friends used to play so happily; now it was a heap of rubble on which grew clumps of stinging nettles and prickly weeds. Climbing over broken bricks and old utensils, she got a feeling she was being watched by something horribly evil. She stood stock still before slowly turning in a full circle, holding the Sword up high.

The upper floors had been reduced to shelves of masonry balanced precariously in the dank, heavy air of the tower. Mairi looked at a piece of broken furniture sticking out from the rock-strewn ground. There was simply nothing left but a feeling of sadness tinged with menace. Rhona had been right. This was a mistake. The girl started to scramble down a slope of shattered stones when a thin, croaky voice called out from above:

"Not so fast, Princess."

Terrified, Mairi stopped and looked up. A wrinkled face peered down from the shelf-like floor of the next storey. It wore a red cap, its eyes were hollow, like the Kelpie's, and two long, pointy teeth jutted from its lower jaw, like an upside-down walrus, pressing against a thick upper lip. She thought the monster resembled the bulldog belonging to a child-catcher who'd once chased her in Glasgow, yet it was more human than dog. In the eerie blue light of the Sword, those yellowed teeth glinted in an evil greenish grin.

"Be a good girl and put that annoying thing down!"

it commanded. The creature leapt from the stony shelf like a cat and landed just yards from where Mairi stood. "If you do as I say it'll be less painful for you when the Humming Bird does his job. Just put down the Sword!"

Mairi already knew she wasn't the only one who could feel fear and something about this part-human creature told her he was also afraid – of the Sword, perhaps?

"Red Cap at your service, Princess. Hungry?"

Red Cap skewed his head to one side. The flickering blue from the Sword played weird patterns on his grotesque face and whenever he opened his mouth to speak Mairi saw a hint of patches of red turned purple staining his fleshy tongue. Someone else's blood?

"No," she said firmly. "And tell me what you've done with my friend."

"Your friend? Do you *have* any friends, Princess?"

"Lots. And you know who I mean," She raised the Sword high. Red Cap, grovelling on all fours and dressed in a red shirt and old-fashioned breeches, backed off.

"You really ought to put that thing away. You're too big to play with toys now. Such a bonnie lass, too! I'll send a crow to fetch him. The Kelpie, I mean."

Mairi stepped forwards. Red flames appeared in Red Cap's deep-set eyes and she halted, as if unable to move any further.

"Good!" exclaimed the monster. "Not as strong as I feared, although by the look of you, you must have reached fifteen. It's why the Kelpie brought you back, right? Just turned fifteen?"

Mairi recalled what Rhona had said about her

sister's fifteenth birthday. She felt confused. What if she *was* that other girl after all and that this had been planned and was meant to happen. She wavered, lowering the Sword. She thought of the magnificence of the great horse and his sorrow that he couldn't enjoy the beauty of those 'flowers' carpeting the plain in front of the lofty palace.

"I... " she began.

Just when she was about to drop the Sword, a small rabbit ran past. The same rabbit? The girl wasn't sure, for all wild rabbits looked alike to her and a ruin such as this might be teeming with bunnies, but when he stopped and gazed up at her she knew to follow him, watchful of Red Cap. The rabbit took her to a spiral staircase that wound down into the ground; she trailed after him, the ghastly sound of Red Cap's breathing close behind.

"Don't go any further!" the monster warned but Mairi ignored him. They entered an underground cavern that stank of toadstools and damp earth. Holding the Sword aloft, she scanned rows of barred empty cages till, in the very last cage, she spied a lone figure slumped forwards on the floor. Dressed in rags, it was a boy of about her age. "He can't help you now! I don't know why the Master didn't do away with him – like he did with his stupid father, the woodcutter."

"Lachlan?" The boy looked up. "It's *me*!"

The boy stood up and stared, puzzled. Red Cap edged away. "Kill him now," ordered the creature. "Kill the miserable boy and I promise the Humming Bird won't hurt you when it happens."

Mairi turned and swiped the Sword at Red Cap who sprang backwards with a snarl, then slunk into a corner.

Open that cage and I might let you live!" the girl commanded.

Keeping his distance, Red Cap crawled past her to the cage, complaining bitterly. Removing a ring of heavy keys attached to its belt, the hideous creature slotted one into the rusty key-hole and opened the door.

"You'll regret this, Princess. When the Master..."

Without warning, the rabbit flew at Red Cap, only he was no longer a rabbit. He'd transformed into a large dog that grew and grew, till it became an enormous hound. The hound bit at Red Cap's legs and the monster, howling with pain, stood on bent hind limbs and began to dance about to avoid the animal's snapping jaws. Mairi darted into the cage, took the bewildered boy by the hand and ran with him to the staircase. Neither looked back, but from the sound of it Red Cap was putting up a fight. Mairi didn't wait to find out who the winner might be. Scaling the spiral stairs, they soon reached the courtyard and, from there, the entrance. They found Rhona hiding behind the trunk of a broad tree. She looked from Mairi to the boy.

"This is Lachlan," the older girl announced, returning the Sword to Rhona.

"How do you know me?" asked the boy. "Have you...? Wait a minute – turn round – your eyes..."

Mairi turned to look at him.

"You don't remember me?"

"It can't be!" exclaimed Lachlan. "Mairi? The Princess? It's true, then?"

Mairi laughed as tears welled up in the boy's eyes.

"I don't know what's true any longer, but yes – I am Princess Mairi. And my friend is Rhona. She saved my life."

"And you mine. Look, we'd better..."

"Come back with us! To the faeries' glade. I'll explain everything."

"Wait... that Sword. It's what my father told me about before they took him away. Something to do with a Sword, he said. On my fifteenth birthday. That was yesterday. He said to come to the tower where you and I used to play together. But it was like I'd walked into a trap – that revolting thing called Red Cap..."

"*This* Sword?" queried Mairi.

"Father just said the Sword of the White Boobrie. With a ruby in the hilt. They were dragging him away. He told me to run. The Ghillie Dhu helped me escape."

"Ghillie Dhu?" asked Rhona, puzzled.

"The dog that held back Red Cap. Sometimes he looks like a rabbit, but he's really a tree spirit. When he needs to he can turn himself into almost anything, but mostly he's pretty shy and hides away in an old hollow birch."

"Oh," replied Rhona for whom anything now seemed possible.

"You look so different!" Mairi said to Lachlan. "It's been such a long time – and I've so much to tell you!"

"*You're* not only different – you're – well – you know," replied Lachlan shyly.

"I know *what*?" Mairi was grinning.

"You're..." Lachlan looked away as if trying to hide a blush. "You're, um, you're, well, very beautiful. You would be of course, being the Princess – but I never thought..."

Mairi took his hand and laughed. Suddenly she stopped and turned serious.

"But your father, Lachlan? Red Cap talked as if

he'd been killed."

"I don't believe it. He knew something – something the Kelpie needed to know – and he'd never give away a secret. Not even under tor–" Lachlan hesitated as though the word was too awful to say. Mairi stroked his hand. "Under torture," he added quietly.

"We'll find him. I promise."

Rhona felt excluded as the two bosom friends of old walked side by side along the forest path back to the faery glade, and more than a little hurt. Although she'd reckoned for some time her sister Caitlin deserved a boyfriend, she never thought it might be like this with her being shut out. She dragged the heavy Sword that no longer glowed behind her.

Suddenly Lachlan stopped and turned.

"That Sword was glowing blue back there by the tower, right?" he asked.

"Always glows blue when I hold it and *Mairi's* in danger." Rhona answered softly, stressing 'Mairi' as though she, Rhona, was of no importance

"May I – um – would you mind if I held it?"

"I don't know about that. I'm the Keeper of the Sword, you see."

"Can't be the same Sword, then. Father said the Sword of the White Boobrie glows white in the hands of the true Keeper. But please let me just..."

"Let him, Rhona. He *was* my best friend once – and now – well, perhaps now he's my second best friend! After you!"

Were they trying to butter her up? Rhona, pouting, handed the Sword to Lachlan. As soon as he took it she jumped backwards in alarm for the Sword flashed a brilliant white; whiter than anything she'd seen before.

"You?" queried Mairi. "You've been the Keeper of the Sword all the time!"

And when Lachlan raised the Sword high above his head the whole forest seemed to light up. Rhona grinned, for she no longer resented the closeness between Mairi and Lachlan. Now their friendship seemed uplifting, like the Sword itself.

"No one is ever going to steal the eyes and soul of my Princess whilst I'm still alive!" the boy yelled at the forest, and for a few moments Rhona sensed the trees and plants around them silently cheer.

They hurried on to the faery glade.

"So you found him?" Fiona said as soon they entered her hut. Once again they were inside an enormous natural cathedral. The faery girl stood preparing breakfast. Her father looked up eagerly from a table.

"Of course she did, Fiona. Otherwise I'd never have let the girls leave."

"You knew?" asked Mairi.

"Knew – and arranged! You don't think it was a real cockerel crowing, do you? We don't eat eggs or chickens!"

"Oh dear! We left the Ghillie Dhu battling with that awful monster, Red Cap."

"Don't worry, Princess. Red Cap's no match against the magic of our faery cousin. Now – come and eat whilst I give the true Keeper of the Sword the knowledge he's going to need."

The two girls sat at the table with Lachlan sandwiched in between. Rhona just prayed she'd one day meet a boy as good-looking as the woodcutter's son. She thought of the pimpled thirteen-year-olds in her class at Earlston High School and shuddered to imagine she could ever end up with a boyfriend as unappealing as any of them. Whenever Lachlan glanced at her she went all jelly-wobbly inside. But by the time she managed to brave a smile he'd be looking the other way and talking again to Mairi. He obviously wanted to know every detail of the other girl's life in the streets of Glasgow in the time of Queen Victoria, but not for the reasons Rhona first suspected.

"Those places you mention, Mairi – Sauchiehall Street – George Square – the Gorbals... tell me about them."

"Okay, but please don't ask me about *that* place – the orphanage in the Gorbals," begged Mairi. "Some girls preferred to end their lives in the River Clyde rather than stay on. Funnily it was always my friends who ended up dead!"

"*Only* your friends? Didn't that strike you as odd? Why did only your friends have to end up in the river?"

Mairi shrugged her shoulders.

"When my *very* best friend drowned I decided to escape," she replied.

"Don't you see? They weren't committing suicide – they were being eliminated. By *him*."

"Who?"

"The Kelpie. The City you describe is his yet he can never go there."

"No! This can't be. The city I came from is called Glasgow. And they have a Queen. She's fat and her name's Victoria. That's all I know about her."

"Same street names? The Gorbals? A big slow-flowing river? It's The City, for sure."

Mairi turned to Fiona as if seeking the truth from someone who knew everything. Rhona could have told her sister-look-alike that Lachlan would only ever speak the truth, but she kept her mouth firmly shut.

"Yes – you describe The City," confirmed the faery. "The fat Queen too. We never go there because it's dark and dangerous but we've heard of those places Lachlan mentions, Princess. And if you were there, the Kelpie would've had every reason to kill all your friends until you became of age."

"Of age? Fifteen?"

"We all knew. Everyone knew. You see, something special was to happen to you both when you became fifteen. You and Lachlan share the same birthday. Remember?"

Caitlin too, thought Rhona. *And she went and fell into a waterfall on her fifteenth birthday... and now I'm a part of it all as well! Just a wee part, worst luck!*

"One of the Kelpie's spies tried to shoot the Queen you speak of – so *he* could..."

"No," insisted Mairi. "We have to be talking about a different place."

"The man failed," continued Fiona, "and that made the Kelpie nervous. You see, if he steals your eyes and soul he can then get into your body and become you, and yet it won't really be you as you are. It'll be him. He'll become Queen Mairi. And as such he can cross over and enter The City as the new queen."

"Would my sister – I mean Mairi – still look the same?" asked Rhona innocently. She'd seen pictures of Queen Victoria and was not amused that either Mairi or Caitlin could ever look like that, but she was taken aback when she saw the anger in Lachlan's eyes. Looking away, he replied:

"No one is ever going to steal the Princess's soul! Understand?" For a moment the Sword flashed so brightly Rhona had to shield her face.

For the rest of the meal, Rhona sat and ate in sulky silence. She heard how Lachlan was certain his father had been taken to The City and was either being forced to work in a poorhouse (Mairi appeared shocked by the suggestion) or kept prisoner somewhere else. Despite her reluctance to return to the city that she knew – Glasgow – Mairi agreed that the woodcutter had to be rescued at all costs. And even Rhona resigned herself to Lachlan's plan if it might make the boy smile at her just once in the same way as he smiled for Mairi.

Chapter 8: Craddick

Craddick and Captain Hokkit both silently prayed for something magical.

At first each gnome leader had only his supporters as the battle raged on in the Palace courtyard. Swords flashed, swung and cut whilst gruff gnome grunts and shrill gnome cries disturbed the air whenever an arrow found its mark or a spear-thrust achieved its purpose. Neither gnome leader had any intention of surrendering as the battle line altered in favour of his opposite number, and after an hour of fighting, with countless gnomes left dead or dying, it still looked like stalemate. Just when it seemed the battle would finally draw to an uncertain close because of total gnome exhaustion on both sides, something extraordinary happened.

A great white bird circled above the Palace then landed on the turret flying the torn pennant. The commotion ceased as a horde of breathless gnomes craned short necks to stare in wonder up at the bird. The White Boobrie cocked his head, fixing individual gnomes with his golden eye; each time, the gnome concerned went completely still. Captain Hokkit pushed one of those affected by the bird's gaze and the soldier fell like a stiffened dummy. He looked around. On realising all the frozen gnomes were on his side, he panicked. Whilst fleeing for the stairway, he tripped on a broken spear. His bulbous nose slammed into the stony ground but no sound of pain emerged from his gaping mouth. He'd become as rigid as the statue of a prancing horse at the far end of the courtyard.

The White Boobrie stretched his great wings, flapped them like shrouds in a breeze then leapt from the turret and rapidly receded into a white point high in the sky before vanishing. Craddick, overjoyed, turned to his gnome followers:

"Take Hokkit down to the dungeon before he wakes up!" he shouted. "And bind all his followers. *I* am now Captain of the Palace Army. Not Hokkit!"

Board-like, Captain Hokkit was carried by two strong gnomes down the stairs and into the dungeon where double padlocks were fitted to the cage door. Jadda, having conveniently switched allegiance, seemed only too happy to stab at his ex-boss with a rat-prod. Back in the courtyard, all those who had supported Hokkit were trussed up like roasting chickens ready before being placed in neat rows. One by one they came to, their alarm evident from bewildered gnome expressions. Craddick, the new captain, walked up and down between the rows.

"Anyone amongst you miserable gnomes still siding with that old fossil, Hokkit?" he asked. Not a single bound gnome budged and most barely dared to blink. "Don't be shy!" continued Captain Craddick. "I can easily arrange for you to join your leader." Not one word emerged from the tightly-closed gnome mouths. "Well – I'd better give you all time to think whilst I decide what to do with that vermin Hokkit. Of course, those who join with me will get gnome privileges when Princess Mairi is crowned Queen. Queen of the Palace *and* Queen of the City." A wave of gnome whispers spread through the ranks of Palace soldiers. "The day has come," continued the captain. "The Princess is fifteen and she *must* become Queen. Nothing can stop this now. Our leader, the Kelpie, knows this and will respect all who helped to get rid of that traitor, Hokkit. He was planning to kill the Queen after the Humming Bird had done his job and take over the Palace himself. Long live the Kelpie!"

Captain Craddick raised his sword in the air and waved it from side to side. Soon, every standing soldier in the Palace courtyard did the same, calling out "Long Live the Kelpie!"

When the noise had died down, one of his more important guards, wearing a large metal helmet (only high-ranking gnomes wore metal helmets rather than pointy felt hats), suggested they keep Hokkit alive and bring him out every so often to make public confessions and swear support for the new leader. Craddick appeared to turn this over in his hairy head before replying:

"Good thinking! Might be of more use alive than dead. I'll get him to bow before me in public –prove loyalty to his commander. And in the City..."

"The City, sir?" questioned the same soldier.

"Yes, the City! Things are going to change big time for us gnomes when Queen Mairi takes over there. Like we'll no longer be confined to garden duty on either side of the wall – as a reward for loyalty to our master... or mistress. We'll be able to live free!" A roar of approval filled the courtyard. Even bound gnomes bumped up and down with excitement on their squidgy bottoms at the thought of freedom at last. "The Kelpie will see to it!" shouted Craddick.

He left his lieutenants poking at, and teasing Hokkit's gnomes before mounting the staircase to the top floor – the royal suite, unoccupied since the King had been so cruelly killed by the Kelpie. The Princess's royal bedroom was just as it had been back then when

Craddick was a mere under-gardener to Hokkit. He ran his finger along the edge of the richly-carved wooden bedstead then peered at it. Not a speck of dust! Every day a team of Palace-cleaning gnomes would swish and rub and polish its way through the suite, fearing for their lives if anything got knocked over or damaged, terrified should ex-Captain Hokkit's inspection reveal any fault. Now all of this was his – Captain Craddick's – to oversee until Princess Mairi could be re-instated in her rightful place as Queen.

He'd met the fifteen-year old Princess and had been bowled over by her beauty. Although still little more than a child, she had a strange power over him that made him respect her. She'd have to be treated with caution as would that other girl picked up by the White Boobrie in that strange world beyond the waterfall.

But what happened in the courtyard? How could any gnome ever have hoped for more; for the magical force of the great White Boobrie to be used in *his* favour? Of course, it was all part of Craddick's plan. And the Kelpie had said the White Boobrie would decide the fate of all in the Palace and the City, although *he* had been referring to the ultimate destruction of the mysterious white bird from the North who challenged his power. Craddick, now serving two masters, wasn't so sure.

What really worried Craddick was the crossover. To travel across to the City too soon might mean getting stuck forever in the garden of some rich, crabby, old Victorian lady – perhaps even that of the fat Queen.

He remembered well the Kelpie's anger when that assassination attempt failed. The man whose bullet missed must have been the sorriest person alive when the Queen pardoned him and sent him off to her 'colonies', for the Kelpie's evil agents would have soon tracked him down and set about turning his life into a hell worse than anything Auld Clootie might have conjured for him in his darkly glimmering world of eternal fiery furnaces and giant bubbling cauldrons. For the time being, Craddick would play along with the deception that the battle between himself and Hokkit had been a personal thing, that *he* was the Kelpie's loyal Captain and that the Kelpie would become the new Queen Mairi with the eyes and the soul of the girl who took the Sword from him.

Craddick set about checking that everything was neatly in place, from the royal dresses and undergarments to brushes and toiletry and books for girls of the right age, and bed-linen. He stopped, pulled out his hanky, sweat-soiled after the toil of battle, and wiped a spattered window with it. He'd have to have a word with the Palace-cleaning gnomes. No more slovenly work would be tolerated under his leadership, for sure. When he was satisfied not one item of importance was out of place, he left the suite and climbed to the turret to await the White Boobrie. Travel by a boobrie, who could come and go across any barrier and into any world, was the only way he might enter the City without ending up in a garden. In the City he would make preparations and the Kelpie would know nothing until the day of reckoning. And in the City he could seek out the true Keeper of the Sword.

***

"Okay," agreed Mairi. "I'll come with you on one condition: that you never for one second leave my side. If I meet one of those child-catchers and you're not with me – I – I just don't know what I'd do!"

Lachlan reached out and stroked the girl's cheek. Rhona looked the other way.

"It won't happen, Princess. I promise. You do believe me when I promise things, don't you?"

Mairi grinned.

"Aye! We were always promising each other things when we were little. I remember. Oh and that daisy chain crown! You said I needed a crown being a Princess and promised to make me one. Next time my father brought me to the tower you put a crown of daisies on my head. I was so excited – but so sad when the flowers withered and died. I thought I would die too – and it was just before..."

"Before your mother got killed?"

"Aye!"

Tears welled in Mairi's eyes and Rhona groaned inwardly when the boy put his arm around her sister to comfort her. She feared he might kiss her. Yuk!

"Look, you've nothing to be afraid of," reassured the boy. "Ever since the White Boobrie saved you and you vanished, I knew you'd return. And I've been practising."

"Practising?"

"With a sword. Well – a stump of wood really, but my friend and teacher, the Ghillie Dhu, always told me that one day – when you came of age – I'd use the real thing. I was heartbroken yesterday morning when that day came and I went to the tower and it was deserted. Our birthdays are on the same day and I'd prayed you would be there. Red Cap caught me unawares and imprisoned me. You just can't imagine how I've felt when you turned up. And how surprised I was. I only remembered you as a little girl. And your friend..."

Rhona's face turned pink when the woodcutter's boy grinned at her. "She looked great as a Sword Keeper, you know."

Is that all? wondered Rhona, going a deeper shade of red.

"Are you sure you're not related!" he added. "I mean, there's something about you both..."

"She's my – um..." began Rhona, hesitant.

"Rhona saved my life!" blurted Mairi. "She's very special."

"Aye," agreed Lachlan. "She's special all right!"

Rhona wasn't sure whether to feel proud, embarrassed or angered. In the end she decided to feel hopeful; hopeful that he meant it not just because she'd saved her sister – or whoever the other girl was. They sat down at a table with Fiona. The faery girl spread out a large map in front of them.

"I don't understand how I could ever read those words, Lachlan," Mairi said sadly, first stroking the word for 'Cathedral' then a rectangular block called 'George Square' and a cluster of houses south of the river with 'The Gorbals' written across them. "That book I lost – I knew the stories through the pictures but the words were just a jumble of letters. My father was teaching me to read before they took him, but I forgot everything in the orphanage. I only knew that I once loved my parents. But now..."

Oh sister! thought Rhona. *You're completely book mad! You never stop reading!*

"Good," said Lachlan. "Because I never got taught either, being a woodcutter's son."

"I'll teach you!" Rhona suggested. Three heads swivelled and stared. "*Both* of you, I mean – if the Princess is – um – okay about it."

"Don't worry," interrupted Mairi hurriedly. "If you can read we'll manage between us. So where do you think your father will be hidden?"

"I'm afraid that..." Lachlan stopped short, reached forward and took the hand of the Princess. "You see – those child-catchers you mentioned – I don't know how to say this, but maybe we'll have to use them to get to him."

"You're not suggesting...?" began Mairi.

Lachlan nodded, slowly, and gave the girl's hand a gentle squeeze.

"It's the only way. Like you said, all your friends in the City were killed. And for a reason. We'll have to use your enemies to help us find him. With the help of the friend here who saved your life."

Mairi glanced at Rhona.

"I'm not putting her life at risk. We'll have to leave her behind."

Rhona's heart sank. How could she ever impress the boy if she wasn't even there?

"As you said, Princess, she's special. Saved your life once and likely to do it again. We might need her."

Rhona positively glowed. "I'll never leave you, sis!" she insisted.

"Sis?"

"Well – we really are like sisters now, aren't we?"

Lachlan took Rhona's hand too. The younger girl thought the ground had opened up and she was about to fall through it. He joined the two girls hands together, placing his own over them, then swore:

"By the Sword of the great White Boobrie I shall protect these two girls with my life, my soul and everything I have..."

"So, *I* know where to go to find the child-catchers,"

interrupted Mairi, "but do *you* know how we can enter the City – assuming it really is Glasgow?"

Fiona answered:

"There's the White Boobrie, but we can't rely on him appearing when needed. Also the waterfall – but only the Kelpie can cross over through the water. Or there's the Hole in the Wall."

"Hole in the Wall?" questioned Mairi.

"Aye. The Wall behind the Palace. Stretches across the mountains and some say it's got no beginning and no ending. If you try to walk round it you could still be walking as a little old lady and be no nearer the end of it. But there's a hole. Not large enough for a fat queen to squeeze through, but you young girls and the woodcutter's boy should manage, I'm sure."

"And gnomes?" asked Rhona.

"And gnomes, if not too tubby. Gnomes happy to spend the rest of their lives in gardens. See – it's here. Near the Cathedral," she added, placing a small finger on the centre of the map.

"The Necropolis?" asked Mairi.

"I don't know what they call it there on the other side, but they say it's where spirits are laid to rest."

"I just pray my father isn't among them," Lachlan whispered.

"I've a feeling he won't be," said Fiona. "And I've a feeling the Kelpie is as keen for you to come looking for your father in the City as you are to find him."

"Why?" the boy asked. Fiona looked in the direction of the Sword standing strong beside the entrance, stuck into the ground like a cross. "You think he wants the Sword back?"

Fiona nodded.

"Sure of it. Had it in his possession since the

Princess vanished all those years ago. *He* knows its true power better than any other creature alive. Some say the White Boobrie transferred so much of his own power into the Sword that he's become weakened. Could be why he's wary. The Kelpie doesn't know of this – and thinks his own strength, even with the Sword, is no match against the White Boobrie's, but he's wrong. At the moment he's far stronger than the magical bird. Even the Humming Bird could destroy the White Boobrie. It's why he's so careful. And remember – the Sword'll show you the way through the Hole."

Later, two girls and a boy left the forest and crossed the plain under the cover of darkness. They followed the mountain trail up and over a steep pass not far from the Palace, now darkly threatening, then down towards a stone wall that stretched as far as they could see in both directions – although that wasn't very far, for the dull, cloud-dappled sky with neither stars nor moon gave no light. A fine, cooling drizzle had made the stony scree slippery as they picked their way between clumps of heather, guided only by the faint glow of the Sword. Above and behind them, the Palace that gleamed white in daylight, balanced high on the cliff, now appeared dark and ominous. They expected showers of arrows to rain down from its battlements and windows, but everything remained enshrouded in an unearthly stillness.

Mairi held the map out and Lachlan lifted up the Sword to help her see.

"What did Fiona mean – the Sword will show you the Hole? How?" She peered with disappointment at the crumpled piece of paper on which the Wall was depicted as a thick, straight line. "This isn't very helpful."

Lachlan took the map, holding the Sword close to it.

"It's got to be somewhere near here," he said. He looked up at the Wall, then back to the map.

An idea hit Rhona in a flash: desperate to impress, she asked Lachlan to hold the map up in front of her.

"No, the other way round," she insisted. The boy turned the map around so it was facing away from the younger girl. "Now hold up the Sword – nearer."

Rhona giggled with excitement.

"There... see! Come round here, Mairi."

airi joined Rhona and together they stared at the reverse side of the map. A tiny pin-point of light showed through a hole in the paper directly over the line of the wall, yet when they turned the paper over and inspected it no hole was to be seen.

"You're brilliant, Rhona!" exclaimed Lachlan.

No one at school had ever called *her* brilliant. Caitlin, yes, but for Rhona, being the sporty one, the term 'brilliant' didn't seem to apply.

"I told you..." affirmed Mairi. "She's my best friend forever! So..."

"Wait," cautioned Rhona, "it'll be like hunt the thimble. Has to be..."

"Hunt the what?"

"The thimble. A game we used to play – remember? No – silly me – that was Caitlin, of course. Look, the closer we get to the Hole in the Wall, the larger the hole in the map. Like it's wanting to say 'warmer' the nearer we are."

"You might be right! Come on, Lachlan. We'll follow Rhona."

Rhona cheerfully skipped off and moments later

stood waiting for the others in front of the Wall.

"Try again," she urged. Lachlan held the map in front of the Sword. The point of light was minute. Rhona walked slowly beside the Wall for a few metres and the light vanished. She retraced her steps and followed the Wall in the opposite direction and the hole in the map got larger and larger. Rhona had never before experienced such elation. Lachlan looked at her as if *she* were the one who'd created the magic. A few more paces and the whole map shone with the light of the Sword. When held up it was invisible but turned the other way there was no hole at all.

"Must be here!" the girl insisted, approaching the Wall.

"Wait!" Mairi advised. "Let Lachlan go first. You've no idea how dangerous Glasgow can be. I'd never forgive myself if anything happened to you."

Funny, thought Rhona, stepping aside; Caitlin always said the same thing whenever Rhona talked about extreme sports she longed to try out one day – mountain climbing, white river kayaking and ski-jumping.

Lachlan went up close to the Wall which looked no different here compared with any other section of it. He patted the cold stone. Solid. He tapped at it with his Sword, making a metallic clunk, then shrugged his shoulders.

"Just a minute..." called Rhona, her excitement fading fast. She returned to where Mairi still stood holding back, turned and glanced at the Palace then, facing Lachlan, ran an imaginary line from the Palace, through herself and onto the Wall. "To the left a bit..." Lachlan side-stepped, tapping at the wall every few inches until Rhona told him to halt. "There! Just has to be!" she contended. Lachlan tapped away, his frustration evident in the force he now used. Nothing happened. Rhona's heart sank like a brick in a deep pool. The woodcutter's boy turned to face the girls and, angry with himself more than anything else, stabbed the Sword into the hard earth. It quivered before a blinding flash illuminated the Wall, the kids and even the mountain on which perched the Palace. In the Wall gaped a hole large enough for a sturdy lad like Lachlan to squeeze through. Rhona started to run towards it but Lachlan hurried after and grabbed her arm.

"Wait – please. Me first. Remember?"

The boy returned for the Sword, now glowing more dimly. He passed through the hole; Mairi followed, then Rhona. As soon as they were on the other side the hole vanished.

"You, Rhona, shall be the Keeper of the Map, ay?" Lachlan winked and Rhona fizzed with happiness.

All three stood side by side in front of a broken tomb with an angel statue. Rhona folded the map and slotted it into the belt around her waist. Orange torch lights flickered down below in the Cathedral Square; otherwise the City was enshrouded in darkness. With Mairi's help, they found a safe hiding place behind a magnificently ornate tomb halfway down the hill. Here they curled up in the long grass and the weeds and fell asleep. Before drifting off, Rhona thought how lucky Mairi was to have a boyfriend like Lachlan, and not only because he was the Keeper of the Sword.

Chapter 9: Dark Winds

All day, Craddick waited at the top of the tower. As the sun sank in the west, dark clouds gathered in the North and slowly approached, enveloping everything with gloom. Still there was no sign of the White Boobrie, yet Craddick was sure this was the right place. Trying to serve two masters was a tiring business for a gnome, so he decided to lie down and take a nap. Besides, the White Boobrie, being magical, would be bound to know where he was. He'd be woken up and taken to The City where he could get on and do what had to be done for another master. Feeling smugly self-satisfied, he snuggled down on the south side of the tower overlooking the plain of trapped souls, sheltered from a strengthening cool breeze that blew from the North.

The gnome was awoken by the sound of howling and flapping. It was still dark. The wind had transformed into a gale and was whistling round the pointed turret, playing with what remained of the pennant, beating at the flag pole in its fury. He sat up and pulled his short cloak about him, beginning to feel cross. Why should he, one time Keeper of the Sword, have to suffer misery like this? He stood and went over to the battlements where he crouched low lest he should be seen by hidden eyes. With Hokkit bound in the dungeon for a reason only he and the previous captain knew, nowhere was safe and he could trust no one. He peered down at the Wall that stretched forever in both directions and at the silhouetted City beyond this. The last time he'd visited the place had been under the protection of the Kelpie's men, gravediggers from the Necropolis, before the Wall appeared. Nobody could explain who built the Wall or why, but it had effectively separated the world of gnomes from that of the humans ever since the King was killed and all his human subjects, save the Princess and the woodcutter's son, turned into flowers now scattered across the plain. Today this would change. The girl was already fifteen.

At first he thought the strange flapping noise came from the torn pennant and the flag-pole, but as it grew and grew the sound seemed wrong. It came from a great black cloud sweeping down from the North – only this wasn't a cloud. From its speed, the way its shape changed and the screaming that now accompanied the flapping, he realised it was a swarm of huge black birds heading straight for the Palace. He tried to hide behind the base of the turret but the swarm encircled the tower so fast he could feel the upward pull of the swirl of air it created, like a mini-tornado. One bird separated from the others and glided down to the tower, landing on a battlement. Craddick wondered how such a huge creature managed to balance there and when he saw the size of its beak, with one fiery red eye fixed on him, he wished he was somewhere else.

Of course the gnome knew precisely why the dark boobries had come for him and his only chance of survival was to play along with the Kelpie's plan: to seek out the Princess and her young friend in The City, pretend to be loyal to the girl's cause and have them lead him to the woodcutter. He approached the beast, studying those cruel talons with trepidation. When he felt he was close enough he stopped and prayed this particular boobrie couldn't read minds as the White Boobrie seemed able to do. In a flash, one of those giant clawed feet left the battlement and scooped up the gnome; enormous wings spread out, and, almost gracefully, the dark boobrie left the tower, clutching the gnome. Craddick too was now part of the deadly cloud that swept over the Wall and on into the City.

***

Rhona was the first to be awoken by a howl of wind, a noise the like of which she'd never before experienced. She cowered against her sister's sleeping body, but on seeing the darkness of the approaching cloud she shook the other girl awake.

"Oh my goodness!" exclaimed Mairi, tugging at Lachlan's arm. The boy stirred slightly. Mairi poked him – perhaps a little too hard.

"Ouch!" he yelped before grabbing the Sword. It shone like a beacon, lighting up tombstones and winged angels.

"Lachlan – that cloud – it's... "

"Not a cloud!" warned the woodcutter's son. "No rain, see! Stay low. They mustn't spot us."

"*They*?"

"Flying devils from the North my father used to call them. The dark boobries."

"Like the..." began Rhona.

"Aye, only black – and as evil as the White Boobrie is good. They mustn't see your pretty dresses. Quick! Crawl under me!"

Lachlan let go of the Sword to dim its light. With no time to seek out a better hiding place, he made a human arch like a gymnast and the two girls crouched together under the protection of his body, their bottoms sticking out. The boy pulled up handfuls of weeds and grass to cover the girls' bottoms until they were sufficiently camouflaged, just before the howling, shrieking black cloud swept past overhead, accompanied by a cold gust that blew away the plants and ballooned Mairi's and Rhona's dresses. To a passer-by it must have appeared as if the woodcutter's son was doing stretches over a couple of colourful exercise balls, but thankfully the black boobries had already moved on, spreading out over The City. Lachlan playfully patted the exercise balls.

"You can come out now!" he chuckled.

The girls crawled out backwards, Rhona's face almost as red as Mairi's hair. Biting her lower lip, she turned away from the boy and stared at the terrifying black birds as they dropped into the dim streets beyond.

"It's not just child-catchers from now on, though perhaps black boobries can turn into child-catchers!" whispered Lachlan. "Neither of you must leave my sight. Understand?"

Rhona nodded before looking away from the boy and into the distance. Did he really care about her, she wondered, or was she just an encumbrance to him and her sister?

"Mairi, as soon as it's light we'll seek out a child-catcher."

"Really?" The red-haired girl's eyes said it all. Even in the presence of Lachlan and the magical Sword, the mere mention of the word sent a shiver down her spine.

"It's the only way. We *must* get to my father. He's our one chance of destroying the Kelpie's power."

"How come?" asked Mairi, searching for any excuse to avoid any encounter with a child-catcher.

"He's just a mortal woodcutter. What can *he* do?"

"It's not so much what he can do as what he knows. And they'll realise that we're looking for him for this very reason. It'll be why Auld Clootie released the dark boobries. To help the Kelpie. The good thing is it means he's not yet strong enough on his own."

"Good?" Mairi was sceptical of the boy's choice of word.

"My sis – I mean Mairi – she's right," chipped in Rhona. "It's much too dangerous to leave her with the child-catchers. What if they *don't* take her to the poorhouse? Suppose the Humming Bird's crossed over into the City already?"

"Rhona – what are you trying to say?"

"Me! Let them take *me* to the poorhouse. Let *me* find him."

Mairi and Lachlan stared at the younger girl, neither quite sure what to make of her suggestion.

"No, Rhona. Far too risky," the boy said at last. "We'll have to come up with another plan. Mairi, do you have any idea where the poorhouse is?"

Rhona looked disappointed for, in her mind, she'd been captured, taken to the poorhouse and had found the woodcutter. Lachlan then burst in, grabbed her (gently, of course) and his father and whisked them away to the Necropolis chased by a swarm of child-catchers, a flock of boobries and with rats and hound dogs racing after them as well, and they'd only just managed to squeeze through the Hole in the Wall in time. There was no Mairi in her mental picture of what could happen. *She* would have stolen Rhona's limelight!

"Near my old orphanage, I'm sure," answered Mairi.

"Is there anyone there who might help us?"

"All too evil – but no, wait – a skinny little lady who worked in the kitchens. Never said a word but used to look really sad whenever I got beaten. She…"

"The orphanage it is, then! We'll scrounge some food there. And do *not* let me lose sight of either of you. *Particularly* you, Rhona!"

Lachlan looked pointedly at Rhona. She wasn't sure what to make of the look. Was it possible he cared more for her than for her sister? If only he'd say something to *her* instead of talking always to Mairi!

"You all right, Rhona?" Mairi asked. "We'd quite understand if you want to go back to the forest to be with the Seelie Faeries. The City's no place for little girls! *I* should know!"

Little girls indeed!

"I'm fine," replied Rhona curtly, eyeing Lachlan.

With a rim of pink dawn light hovering over the sleeping City, a woodcutter's boy and two girls slunk down the hill to the Cathedral Close then, with Mairi in the lead, continued through the early morning streets, running in short bursts, hiding in doorways whenever they spotted other silent souls. On reaching the orphanage, Mairi held back. It was a few years since she'd last felt the rod of that sour-faced bitch of a warden across her back but the mental scars it left had never properly healed. Lachlan placed a comforting arm around her shoulders and Rhona looked the other way.

"Is the kitchen at the side of the building?" he asked.

"Aye!" answered the older girl. "The kitchen lady will be there now. Preparing the porridge. Picking out the cockroaches as best she can. She always tried hard, you know. To be kind. I only pray she's still alive."

Lachlan led her by the hand to the side of the dreary, grey-brick orphanage. A door was half-ajar, and from the other side of it the splash of water, the clatter of metal plates and another sound: that of a woman humming a sad, haunting tune.

***

Craddick clung to the dark claws of the boobrie, although he need not have; not even a steel wrench could have prized apart those curls of iron-hard horn. Gripped like a garden ornament in the fist of a gardener from Hell, the gnome sped over the Necropolis and the Cathedral before being whirled in diminishing circles as he and the flying beast descended into a spacious square surrounded by big buildings. Even in the dark, he could tell they must be important. After Craddick was released from those claws, the dark boobrie stepped back, its flaming red eye trained on the trembling gnome. The bird lowered its head and craned a long neck forwards. Craddick covered his beard with his big hands, fearful that those flaming eyes, now so close, might set it on fire. As with the White Boobrie, no speech was necessary. That eye seemed to bore into his head and leave messages in his brain:

"Find out from the woodcutter? Find out what?" the gnome questioned.

The boobrie's beak opened and the creature let out a hiss, a cross between the noise of a snake and a steam engine. Craddick backed away.

"A secret? Why does the master...? OUCH!"

A large clawed foot slashed at the gnome's face, catching his bulbous nose. He cupped a shaky hand to his face, saw blood on it then dabbed at his nose with his beard. The answer to his question was written across his mind as clearly as if scribbled on a piece of paper and held in front of his eyes.

The woodcutter would no longer be alive if the Kelpie knew his secret!

With its eye of cold fire boring into the gnome, the boobrie stretched wide two black-shroud wings and leapt into the air, up and over the grim buildings, to join searching, swooping black brothers.

Craddick cursed the White Boobrie for insisting he should pretend he was still working for the Kelpie. He wished he'd had the courage to tear off a piece of the boobrie's wing to hide his gnome clothes, for nothing now could have been worse than the thought of getting picked up as a gnome and turned into the garden variety of his kind. Knowing that boobries, both black and white, had threatened him with such a fate should he fail in his mission was little comfort since at the end of the day only one master could be faithfully served – unless his plan were to work.

Looking up at the sky alive with swirling, swooping dark boobries, it did appear that odds were stacked in favour of the Kelpie and the dark forces of Auld Clootie. But nothing was definite, except that one day even the Princess would change into an ugly old hag.

Unless...?

Either way Queen Mairi would rule. Should the White Boobrie defeat his dark brethren, she'd sit on the throne as herself; if the Kelpie were victorious, then he'd take her eyes, her soul and perhaps even reshape her body for himself. She'd still be Queen Mairi, but as an immortal spirit perhaps she'd never grow old. There again, what warmth would remain in her stolen soul? The girl who took the Sword from him had a true warmth of spirit about her.

Still rubbing his nose, Craddick spied a pile of rubbish. He sauntered over to it and kicked at bits of mouldy food, a dead pigeon and torn clothes until he found a discarded sack cloth just large enough to wrap around his squat, gnomely body and with enough spare to cover his head. As a walking sack, he left the square. Tired and miserable, he spied a cat lying stretched out on the steps of an old church – dead. For the rest of the night he kept company with the rotting corpse of the cat for the smell was so awful no one would wish to approach him.

Being a gnome, he knew little about what happened inside churches but there was a pleasant aura about the place. He'd had the same sort of good feeling when he was with those two very special girls: the one with red hair, the Princess, and the younger one with fair hair. A warm, non-scary feeling. The White Boobrie made him feel that way too, but the Kelpie, who terrified him, also promised things, wonderful things, and threatened him too with terrible things if he were to put a foot wrong. Still unable to decide which master and which boobrie to follow – white or black – he drifted off to sleep.

***

"Holy Mary, Mother of God, forgive me my sins!" cried the old kitchen woman, dropping to her knees and crossing herself when the figure of a boy, lit by an unearthly glow, appeared in the doorway.

Lachlan had gone on in alone, Mairi refusing to enter until she was certain the warden wasn't lurking somewhere behind a door ready to drag her away and beat her. The boy felt upset to see the poor woman grovel so. What evil, he wondered, had turned her into such a wretched person of pity who, through fear, now prostrated herself before a peasant lad? He reckoned Mairi had been right to be scared of the orphanage.

"Please – we've only come to ask for your help," reassured Lachlan. "This Sword I carry is to protect the likes of you. Good people who have no wish to harm anyone. May I and my two friends have a quiet word with you?"

On seeing the boy's kind eyes, the fear in the old woman's heart melted. She nodded and took Lachlan's hand when he offered to help her up. He led her to the outside door where the girls stood waiting. Mairi was trembling.

"Annie?"

"Mairi – little Mairi? Is it really you?" Tears began to trail down the woman's hollowed cheeks. Mairi grinned and took Annie's hands, her own eyes also moistening.

"Yes... it's me all right."

"I feared you were dead. I cried for days... in fact I never stopped crying inside after you were gone. I prayed and prayed to the Holy Virgin to take care of you – and, oh, the Lord be praised, you've come back! And who's this angel with you?" Annie turned to Rhona. "An angel who looks so troubled, the poor wee child!"

Troubled? Rhona glanced at Lachlan. *How could she ever understand how troubled I am? And who cares, anyway?* She forced a smile for the old kitchen help, desperately hoping that Lachlan also thought she looked like an angel.

"Just Rhona," replied the younger girl. "B –" She was going to say 'boring little Rhona' when the woman pulled her by the arm.

"Quick – into the pantry. But..." Annie glanced anxiously at the glowing Sword. "What about that thing?"

"The time's come, Annie. I'll explain when we're safe from prying ears."

They followed the wizened lady along a corridor, through the kitchen that smelt of old cabbages and burnt grease into a tiny cubicle just large enough for all of them to squeeze into surrounded by sacks of oats and potatoes.

"Wait here," Annie said. She disappeared and Rhona blushed in the darkness of the pantry because she felt herself pressed up against Lachlan and he didn't move away. The woman soon returned with a lit candle and closed the door behind her. Rhona stepped aside.

"Oh Mairi – how you've grown! But tell me – where have you been all these years? And that dress? Why, you look like a princess. You're so..."

"She *is*!" interrupted Lachlan. "Always has been. That's the point!"

"What do you mean?"

"I think she was sent here when little – when they killed her father the King – to become strong..."

"Oh, you were always strong in spirit, Mairi. That's why they used to – oh, I got so angry when they beat you. And I felt so helpless! But he said 'King'? Queen Victoria's been on the throne since long before you were born..."

"The other side of the Wall," explained the boy. "In the big Palace. Princess Mairi and I were the best of friends till..."

"I always knew you were different, Mairi," Annie

cut in, "but this boy with gentle eyes and a sword. Is he a prince?"

"No," chuckled Mairi. "A woodcutter's son."

"*I* think he's a prince!" announced Rhona. Lachlan and Mairi turned to stare at her then laughed. Not unkindly, but Rhona took offence. "I do! Honest!" she added, looking away.

"He's the Keeper of the Sword," Mairi continued. "A magical Sword. And we have to find his father. He's here somewhere in the City..."

"Glasgow?"

"Aye... Glasgow. For those on the other side of the Wall it's just the 'City'. First they told Lachlan that his father was dead – but, you see, they need him alive. They didn't want anyone to come looking for him before, but because I'm fifteen it's different now. You see, he knows something that we have to find out. *They'll* try to stop us. The thing is they also want to know what he knows. But Lachlan thinks he would never tell them – it's why he believes his father's still alive."

"I'm sure I don't understand a word of what you just said, little Mairi – well, not so little now – but I'd do anything for you. So... a real princess, ay?"

"Don't feel like one! Not after that night we spent on the Necropolis."

"You spent a night there? Why, shame on you Master..."

"Just Lachlan, if you please."

"*Master* Lachlan! How could you?"

"We had to stay hidden. Because of the dark boobries."

"The what? Oh, you must all be starving! Porridge! I insist."

"We really ought to..." began Lachlan

"Please!" interrupted Mairi. "Annie's porridge is very special!" she informed the boy.

Old Annie gave her a hug and returned to the kitchen. Soon they were sitting squashed together on the floor tucking into bowlfuls of steaming porridge and drinking from mugs of milk. Rhona kept glancing sideways at the woodcutter's son. Her eyes shone with that continuing question: *'Am I really an angel?'* But he gave no answers and she felt sad and unwanted.

"My nephew used to be in the poorhouse," Annie announced out of the blue. "I know that's where they were going to take you, Mairi, before you ran away. They used to talk about you all the time, see. I thought back then it was because you annoyed them with that spirit of yours, but now I understand. Also why they always told me you needed feeding up. They didn't want you to die on them."

"What about all my friends, Annie? What really happened to them?"

"Bad influence, I overheard the mistress say. I thought they meant *you* on *them* – but now I see it was the other way around. Those poor girls always ended up floating in the Clyde. And I knew they hadn't killed themselves. It's why I told the other girls to avoid you when I realised. I'm so sorry!"

"Don't blame yourself, Annie. I'm glad you warned the other girls against me. Might have saved some of their lives. But where can we find your nephew now?" asked Mairi.

"Jamie McTavish. You might remember him. Works for a baker. Brings the bread here and also to the poorhouse every morning. The only time I see him. He may seem a hard man but it's because of what he's been through. He'll take you there for sure."

They didn't have to wait long but it was already light when they set off with Jamie, the dour baker's assistant. Lachlan scanned the heavens for more dark boobries. Nothing! The wind had dropped and the sky was blue; a strange, deep blue that reminded Rhona of the sea in Greece where she and Caitlin and their parents had gone on holiday in a different dimension the previous year. How she'd loved that holiday and the warmth of the water, and how she and Caitlin had laughed when a Greek youth boldly told Caitlin, in broken English, she was 'beautiful like a goddess'. He'd probably never seen a girl with hair that colour before. Back then, boys were a challenge to Rhona because they could sometimes run faster than her and do more daring things, but of late she'd actually *wanted* them to out-run her – and now there was Lachlan.

The streets were already busy with scruffy urchins running about and shouting, women carrying things and scolding the children and men arguing between themselves and with the women. They were noisy and stinky too. Rhona had to pick her way round piles of rubbish and excrement as she followed the girl who looked like her sister and the boy who looked like a young Hollywood star.

The more she thought about things the more it seemed to Rhona she was caught up in a movie. In movies, good things would always happen sooner or later – like a young girl getting rescued by the Hollywood heart-throb. She had nothing against this sister-lookalike Mairi, but if the older girl was truly a princess there could never be a thing between her and Lachlan, a mere woodcutter's son. As the distance between Rhona and the others grew, a plan formed in the younger girl's head. She smiled to herself because she could see it happening there in the cinema of her mind and it was simply delicious. Better than Annie's porridge, any day. As soon as the boy became aware she was no longer with them he'd come running back for her. That's when she would throw herself to the ground and fake injury and he'd take her up in his arms and... oh!

She wasn't sure about the kissing bit. That could come later, she reckoned. But there was also her lovely blue dress which matched the sky and her eyes. Had he noticed that? The same colour as her eyes? Caitlin and Mairi's were greenish. Surely he preferred blue.

Of course she never planned to let the others out of her sight. Besides, she could not get completely lost wearing that posh blue dress in a city of grey...

Chapter 10: The Orphanage

Jamie McTavish squinted anxiously at the Sword before it got shrunk into a dagger that Lachlan slotted into his belt. The boy's right hand remained firmly over the handle, covering the glowing ruby. The baker's assistant had no wish to be on the wrong side of the oddly-dressed lad but the girl fascinated him.

His aunt had told him she was a princess and that he should do everything she told him to do. She was indeed very pretty, but he still thought of her as the red-haired waif who'd run away from the orphanage. He could understand why his aunt was so upset when she disappeared, but to come back, now calling herself a princess, made no sense. Forcing Jamie to risk the wrath of the baker by taking them to the poorhouse when he was still needed back at the bakery had involved a lot of persuasion. It was the Sword that finally did it: the way it glowed and grew and shrank it was surely magical.

"That building there!" he announced after they turned a corner. He pointed to a long, drab, grey building with a single door, its windows all boarded up. Smoke plumed from two tall chimneys, merging with the blue sky. "Won't take one step closer myself. It's *worse* than Hell inside. I'd rather die and end up in the real Hell than go back to that place!"

"But surely you only remember..." began Mairi.

Jamie cleared his throat and spat on the ground. "Princess or no princess, you cannae force me to go any further. Not even if he waves that... that *thing* of his at me he's got stuck in his belt. You make your own way from here on, lass."

Mairi held back. She, too, was reluctant to take one more step towards the building the very mention of which used to strike terror into the street children of her home city of Glasgow. Jamie ran off and Lachlan took her hand on seeing a shadow of terror cloud her face. They were both so distracted they failed to notice that Rhona was no longer following them.

"You'll be safe with me, Princess," reassured Lachlan. "I really have been practising my swordsmanship. Father would be proud, I'm sure of it. *And* your father, the King. If he only he could see me from heaven."

Thus two lifelong friends crossed the street and walked on towards the poorhouse with a single purpose: to find the old woodcutter and learn his secret. Neither Mairi nor Lachlan considered what they might do with the knowledge, or when and how they might return to the Palace to challenge the Kelpie.

***

Craddick awoke with a start. A small urchin boy stood holding his nose and staring at him.

The street was already filled with bustling city dwellers. He growled at the boy, who ran off, then got up from his resting place and wrapped the sack-cloth about his squat little body. Thankfully there was not a single boobrie up above, nor any other sort of bird. How odd, the gnome thought. Maybe ordinary birds had been scared away.

After dusting himself down, Craddick continued in the direction taken by the little urchin away from the posh buildings and hopefully towards the poorhouse.

He was almost bowled over when a young man in

a tearing hurry bumped straight into him.

"Mind where you're going, sir!" he grumbled in his gruff, gnomely voice. The man stopped, eyeing Craddick with suspicion. "Um – you look shabby enough to me! Tell me, where's the poorhouse?" asked the gnome.

"Why d'you want to ken?" responded Jamie. "No one in their right mind would wish to go to that place? Are you with...?" He turned and pointed to a girl with long fair hair he'd just run past. "...with *her* lot?"

Craddick recognised Rhona immediately.

"Thank you, my young man!" he said to the baker's assistant. "You do me a great service!"

Jamie took off again and the gnome approached Rhona.

"The Sword?" he asked. "You have it hidden?"

The girl nearly jumped out of her skin. She'd been wondering where to hide so that Lachlan would easily find her as soon as he noticed she was missing – *if* he noticed. She was beginning to have doubts in this spooky place. It was nothing like the Glasgow that she, Caitlin and their mum went to for a Christmas shopping spree two years back. Buchanan Street had been magical.

"Craddick?" she questioned the bulbous nose and the white beard – all that showed of the gnome through a gap in the sack-cloth.

"Indeed! You have the Sword hidden?"

"No – I gave it to – you see..."

"To Captain Hokkit?" The gnome sounded angry.

"No! Lachlan. He's the true Keeper, you know. The way it lit up in his hand – it was like..."

"Stupid girl! Why?" Rhona backed away from his anger.

"No – Lachlan really *is* the Keeper of the Sword. Only I don't think..." She was about to say 'I don't think my sister really appreciates him' when the gnome sprang forward, grabbed her arm and pulled her into a doorway. Moments later, she saw why. Three aircraft-sized black birds swept down from the sky and shot past. Screaming women and children scattered in alarm.

"We can't stay here!" warned Craddick. "They'll soon find us. You'd stand out a mile away in that blue dress. Must get to the poorhouse – quick!"

"Aye – it's where we were going to... to find Lachlan's father. Me and the others."

"The old woodcutter?"

"Lachlan's certain they've locked him up in the poorhouse. I was following. From a safe distance. He didn't want any harm to come to me in particular, you see," she lied. "He's very caring!"

After the dark boobries had vanished over the rooftops, Rhona and Craddick weaved their way through the panicking crowd to the corner round which Mairi and Lachlan had disappeared. Opposite stood the menacing poorhouse. The Princess and the woodcutter's son were nowhere to be seen and the street ahead was strangely deserted. Obviously nothing would persuade those frantic men and women running about behind them to go anywhere near the place for their terror of the poorhouse was even greater than their fear of the giant black birds. If Rhona had the merest inkling of what went on within those windowless walls she, too, would have turned and fled, but confident that Lachlan would come to the rescue, whatever horror might await her, she walked on – slowly.

Craddick remained where he was. The dark boobries had been a sign. Although this wasn't the Princess, the fair-haired girl would do for the time being. And when she was half-way across the street he turned to check, then nodded...

***

Lachlan banged on the door, there being no bell or anything else with which to announce his arrival. He held the Sword, reduced to the size of a pencil, in a tight fist. Mairi stood right behind him.

"Rhona's missing," she whispered. "I think we should go back for her. She must've got scared."

"Too late! There's someone the other side of the door. I'll not be turning my back on them."

"But..."

"Shhh!"

A giant bolt made a clunk as metal hit metal. The door eased open a crack . Lachlan immediately pushed his way in and grabbed a frail woman who stood alone in the doorway. Behind her was a dim corridor lined by other doors with tiny barred windows, merging with the darkness beyond.

"Where is he?" demanded Lachlan. The woman looked in panic from Lachlan to Mairi. "My father! I know he's here somewhere. Take me to him!" Lachlan gripped a handful of the woman's filthy smock and half-lifted her off the ground.

"Wh-What are you talking about? And who *are* you? This is a p-poorhouse. The girl..." she nodded at Mairi in her fine purple dress. "She's anything but poor."

"She'll be worse than poor if you don't help me find my father. Which way? Where are all the men?"

"Out in the yard breaking rocks. For the roads. The

105

men get up early. Not like those lazy bairns."

"Yard?" Lachlan's free hand rested on the Sword-turned-dagger in his belt. The woman, pressed up against the wall, was staring anxiously at it.

"Follow me," she said.

With the Princess holding onto the boy's arm, they were taken along the corridor and into a vast refectory hall. On one side scruffy children sat in silence at long wooden tables, packed together like sardines; a large, hunch-backed woman dressed in black passed between the tables pushing a trolley, stopping now and then to ladle grey mush from a steaming pot into bowls and far too engrossed in her work to notice them. Behind her stalked a gaunt figure with a face like a skull, holding what looked like a whip. The reason for the silence was obvious, but it was eerie to see so many people crowded together without a single word spoken. The other half of the hall was packed with women in blue and white striped dresses and smocks, already hungrily spooning the same grey stuff into their mouths. The only sound was the occasional scrape of a spoon when an inmate tried to collect the last flecks of meal to quell her hunger – a sound that caused the man with the whip to stop and turn and scan the lowered heads for signs of guilt.

Maybe the man knew who the girl in a fine purple dress really was, or perhaps the anger in the boy's eyes unnerved him, but for some reason he asked no questions when the old lady, the beautiful red-haired girl and the sturdy woodcutter's son passed between the rows of women and children towards a door at the far end of the refectory. He merely stood and stared with cold hollow eyes. Mairi avoided his gaze, fearful that by just catching his eye she might feel the sting of his whip. It looked far worse than the rod the orphanage warden had used across her back and she was thankful to leave the hall.

They followed another dingy, stinky corridor (this one smelt of vomit) to a double door which the old lady opened. Sunlight cascaded in and Mairi stood shielding her eyes whilst gazing at an open space teeming with toiling men. In contrast to the hall, the yard was a noisy place: ear-splitting thuds of rocks being smashed with huge, two-handed stone hammers, blended with groans and cries of pain, cut by the occasional scream whenever one of those whip-yielding brutes vented his scorn on an inmate.

"Earning their food and free board," commented the old woman. "Thank the Lord I'm too ill and old to work! I'm not one of *them*, you know. The wardens. Been here since I was a child myself."

Lachlan removed the dagger from his belt. It glowed only faintly.

"Stay with this woman," he told Mairi. "Can't see Father so I'll have to extract the truth out of one of those monsters with whips!"

Mairi watched open-mouthed, her heart racing, as the boy confronted a bully twice his size – a brute whose curled whip seemed little more than a plaything in his enormous hands. The old woman looked worried too. Both feared for the boy, but when the Sword shot to full size, glowing with a blinding light, Mairi turned to the woman and smiled.

"We've been friends since we were little, you know," she said proudly.

"Indeed, my dear. But maybe they've..."

"Shhh! Something's happening"

The man with the whip was shaking his head.

From the expression on his gormless face and the way his eyes fixed on the Sword, Mairi could tell he'd rather be nodding than shaking it. Lachlan shrank the Sword and returned. He looked glum.

"Not here!" he announced. "Has been, but that idiot says he got too weak to work and they took him away. I don't believe him. My father would never give up. He'd work till he dropped if he had to. They must have known I was coming."

"You could try the sick room."

"Where's that?" Lachlan asked.

"In the children's block. It's where most of the children end up before..."

There was a commotion at the far end of the yard. A fight had broken out and one of the inmates was swiping at the legs of another with his hammer. "We'd better leave. Anything can happen here. This is no place for a girl."

But before they reached the door something else froze all three: a blood-curdling shriek high in the sky. A gigantic black bird circled above the yard, joined by another then a third. As each bird descended it turned into a human figure, dark cloaked and carrying a large net.

"What the...?" began the woman in horror.

"We've been seen, Mairi. Quick!"

Pandemonium broke out as the metamorphosing birds touched ground, and Lachlan and the Princess fled to the building. They ran along the corridor and the boy opened the first door they came to: a dark cupboard full of crates and boxes. They closed the door and crouched low. Lachlan tapped the ruby on the hilt of the Sword thrice, slipped it inside his pocket to kill the light and they waited.

"Child-catchers?" whispered Lachlan.

"Yes – only they never used birds when I lived here before. Things have changed."

"They're desperate. They... shhh! Someone's out there. Get behind that crate!"

The sound of approaching footsteps stopped level with the cupboard. No sooner had they got down behind the crate, with Lachlan fingering the tiny Sword, than the door opened.

"Only a stupid cupboard," growled a gravelly voice. Mairi wondered whether its owner had swallowed a mouthful of stones.

"Search it anyway!" demanded another voice. Mairi held her breath.

"And waste time? You heard what the Kelpie said would happen if we don't find out soon. They'll have gone to the children's hall – for the littler one."

The littler one?

There was a loud bang when one of the child-catchers kicked the crate behind which cowered Mairi and Lachlan. The crate jerked backwards and caught Mairi's fingers. The pain was excruciating and the poor girl struggled to control a scream. She clenched her teeth and screwed up her eyelids. The men left, slamming the door behind them. Tears trickled from Mairi's closed eyes. Lachlan hurriedly removed the Sword and held it aloft like a torch.

"Give me your hand," he whispered.

The girl offered her injured hand and winced as Lachlan examined it. Her fingers were badly bruised and there was blood. She watched anxiously as he lightly stroked each finger with the point of the Sword. Magically, the bruising vanished, the blood as well.

"How did you do that?" she asked. "You never told

me you were a magician!"

Lachlan lifted her hand and turned it over to make sure he'd left no hurt bits unfixed.

"I'm not!" he grinned "It's you that's magical. I think we should wait a while."

"But what about Rhona? He talked about the 'littler one'. Maybe that's her. What would she be doing in the children's hall? I couldn't bear it if they've hurt her. She really is special to me."

"Let me think. What happens there?"

"It'll be where they work the children to death. Like the men in the yard, only with work that children can do till they drop."

"They must know she's special for you. Someone must have told them. Perhaps Auld Clootie himself."

"Or the Kelpie. I think he wants to get even more powerful than the Clootie One. It's why he's after my eyes and my soul. I can feel it when I'm near him – and the worst thing is I want it to happen then. It's awful. As if he's already got my soul in his grasp. I…" Tears now streamed her cheeks and Lachlan held her close.

"Never!" he said, stroking the small hand that had been crushed and made better again. "There are other forces. You do feel those too, don't you?" Mairi nodded. "And that thing only my father knows. Think – why is the Kelpie so keen to find out what this is? He has his weakness, Mairi. And you, my Princess, have your strength. Don't forget that! He'll fear you as much as you fear him."

They sat in silence for a very long while, Lachlan's arm around Mairi, the Sword a dagger torch in his free hand. Only when the boy felt certain the corridor was clear did he push open the door and peer out. Taking

Mairi by the hand, he led her away from the cupboard, staying close to the wall. With the Sword extended to full length, he checked every room behind every door until...

Chapter 11: Oakum and Crushed Bones

Rhona screamed. Caught in a large net, she was being yanked backwards so forcefully that she stumbled. Hands grabbed her arms from behind then bound her wrists. She couldn't even properly see her dark captor as she got pushed on towards the building.

"Let go, you beast!" she cried, struggling, but a strong hand kept jamming into her back, jerking her forwards and, still entwined in the net, she staggered on. The black-cloaked figure pushed her along a narrow lane at the side of the building till they reached a dirty red door with peeling paint. A big hairy fist appeared from behind her shoulder and banged on it. Moments later, the door creaked open. A large hunchbacked woman stood before Rhona, legs astride. She had knife-slit eyes and grey caterpillar eyebrows and wore a black dress. She folded her chubby arms and cocked her head at Rhona.

"The girl's got yellow hair! Are you colour blind?"

"She'll do," said a gruff voice behind Rhona.

"Do you call that red hair? Pfff!"

"I'm telling you, this one will do for now. They crossed over together. You should even get some work out of her before... you know!" The chuckle that followed sent a chill down Rhona's spine. It reminded her of icicles falling off the garage roof back home the previous winter.

Oh, how she now missed her parents – and Caitlin! Whatever was going on between Mairi and Lachlan, the girl they all called the Princess was definitely her sister, and yet at the same time she wasn't. And Lachlan? She, Rhona, had always been the

one who'd gone on at Caitlin for not having a
boyfriend, but why did it have to be Lachlan? Why
couldn't she fall in love with someone else?

"Anyway, that posh dress of hers should fetch you
a few pennies!" said the woman.

The net got whisked up off Rhona's head. With
the girl's wrists still tied, the big woman pulled her
into the poorhouse. The door slammed shut behind
her and Rhona never did get to see the face of the
child-catcher. The woman squeezed her arms to check
her muscles were capable of hard labour. It reminded
her of her mother kneading dough. Rhona, fuming,
wanted to say she was top in most sports at school but
decided to stay quiet. When her chance of escape came
she'd be able to run faster than anyone in the building
– she prayed. Better they didn't know this.

A large key hung by a chain from the poorhouse
warden's waist. The woman slotted this into the
keyhole and twisted it. Rhona was now locked inside.

"Turn around!"

Rhona wanted to kick her, snatch the key and
escape from the building, but the warden appeared
unnaturally strong. With eyes narrowed, the girl
turned reluctantly. Her wrists were untied and she
rubbed them as she followed the big woman along the
corridor.

"Too late for breakfast but you've fine muscle on
you! We'll set you to work before the others come
through. There's a couple started already. They're on
no food for two days after a whipping – got caught
trying to steal bread under their skirts, the little
thieves!"

Rhona was taken to a wide, high-ceilinged room
packed with rows of tables laden with tarred ropes and

large, sharp metal spikes. Beside each table were empty baskets. Two young girls in grey smocks, one barely ten, looked up at her.

"Fill two of those baskets with oakum and you may get some lunch, Miss Whoever-you-are!" commanded the warden.

"What's...?" began Rhona.

"Did I ask you to speak?"

Rhona shook her head.

"Two baskets! You can begin whilst I go to fetch the others – the ones with food in their bellies. Must get two more basketfuls from each and every one of you before we move on to bone-crushing."

The woman left. Rhona joined the two girls.

"You'll not survive without vittles," warned the smaller one.

"Without what?" whispered Rhona.

"Vittles. Breakfast, lunch, you ken!"

"Oh!"

Rhona suddenly felt very hungry. It seemed a lifetime ago when she and Mairi and Lachlan had eaten with the Seelie Faeries in that magical forest. Her stomach was crying out for food.

"Here, take one of these," the younger girl said handing Rhona a length of tarred rope. "I'm Polly, by the way. And this is Megan. Never says a word, does Megan. Too frightened."

"Hello. I'm Rhona. But I'm not supposed to be here. I'm really from..."

"No one is *supposed* to be here! But it's where you end up if nobody in the world cares about you. But *we* care for each other – don't we, Megan?"

Megan nodded and glanced shyly at Rhona.

"But *I've* got a family," protested Rhona. "A mum

and dad. *And* a sister. And they *do* care. Very much!"

Polly stared at her then giggled.

"Where did you steal that posh dress from? Is that why you're here then? To save you from a hanging? Should be grateful you're still alive. Use this!" The child picked up a vicious-looking spike. "And be careful with it or you'll end up in the sick room."

"Sick room?"

"Sick room! Never known anyone come out of there alive. Now get to work before the Highland Moo returns."

Rhona smiled.

"Highland Moo? I thought *they* were supposed to be friendly?"

"Not this one! Just watch me. Hold the rope like this and tease out the oakum. You can wipe the tar from your hands on my smock. You'll not want to dirty your dress or the Highland Moo will turn into a Bull! She'll be hoping to get a pretty penny for that dress of yours when you're gone – unless you mess it up. Just toss the oakum threads into your basket. And thank the Lord you're not grinding bones yet."

"Grinding bones?"

"You are ignorant! Bones. Over there in the corner."

Rhona peered over her shoulder. Sure enough, up against a wall was a heap of rotting bones, the cause of the foul smell that filled the room.

"How do you grind them?" asked Rhona, took a thick piece of rope and turned it over a few times as she wondered where to stab it with her spike.

"With a grinder, silly!" Polly gave her friend a 'we've-got-a-right-one-here' look and shrugged her shoulders. "It's not the work of grinding. That's a lot easier than spiking oakum and you don't get tar all over your hands. No, it's the hunger that does it! When you smell that marrow – it's delicious! Mostly you can't stop yourself, see: from sucking out the marrow when you think the Moo isn't looking. Trouble is she's got eyes in the back of her head. And a stick that follows those eyes around. So I hope for *your* sake we don't finish the oakum before lunch! Won't make any difference to me and Megan, though. We've got used to being starved."

Even if she were close to starvation, Rhona could never put one of those bits of dead cow bone anywhere near her mouth.

"Why are we doing this?" Rhona asked as she stabbed at the rope. "I mean what's this stinky stuff for?"

"Oakum? For the ships, they say. Other things too. And the bone-crushing for the crops. To give us food in our bellies, we're told. *When* they feed us!"

"Fertiliser?" queried Rhona.

"Dinnae ken! Shhh, I hear them coming! Get to work. Here – put this lot in your basket." The girl bent down, picked up a handful of oakum and reached across the table. "I like you, Rhona," she whispered. "Dinnae ken why, but I like you. Please don't die!"

Rhona poked and pulled with the spike, teasing out strands of oily fibre which she dropped into her basket. The door opened and the Highland Moo entered followed by a long line of scared-looking scruffy girls of all ages from tots to fifteen-year olds like Caitlin. They gathered around the tables in silence and started to work away with their spikes and lengths of rope whilst the Moo headed straight for Rhona. Her disappointment at seeing the amount of work the new girl had got through was obvious from her expression. When the woman turned away Polly winked at Rhona.

Rhona soon devised a plan for which she secretly thanked a small tot who asked leave to go to the toilet. She had guessed where the toilet was from the smell – up above, off a balcony reached by a spiral metal staircase.

"If there are any other girls who want to waste my time with a visit to the wee room, tell me now – or feel my rod later!" bellowed the Moo.

"Yes, please," Rhona asked politely.

"Go! You've worked well – so far!"

As she climbed the steps, Rhona planned moves she'd learned in gymnastics. She only ever competed in sport to win but this would be one gymnastic event she could ill afford to lose. She didn't need the toilet but she went anyway – her mum always said 'go when you can'. On the way down the steps she completed the most daring gymnastic sequence ever: a forward tumble on a spiral staircase, springing back up, flipping to one side, a head over heels, a slide, another spring before landing face down on the floor. With her head twisted sideways, she watched the Moo from a half-open eye whilst maintaining the glazed expression of a china doll, faking concussion. It worked. The horrified woman stared, fearing perhaps a girl in her charge had just fallen to her death, although Rhona guessed that the look was more about worrying her blue dress might have got spoilt. She closed her eyes when the Moo approached. A stubby finger poked into her back and she gritted her teeth against the urge to giggle. An outburst of laughter could have earned her a flogging.

"Fetch the stretcher, someone. I'll need three

strong girls to take this stupid child to the sick room. You two, Polly and Megan – and one other – run for the stretcher."

Thankfully the Moo made no further attempt to find out whether Rhona was alive or dead. The girl allowed herself to be rolled onto the stretcher. She caught Polly's anxious eye; although wishing to inform the other girl, 'I'm fine – don't worry – I'm a gymnast!' she stayed as still as a corpse. Borne aloft along dingy corridors, a thought gnawed at her mind: what if Polly knew something she didn't know about the sick room, something unmentionably awful? Maybe she'd made a bad decision, but she couldn't allow negative feelings to spoil her triumph. For Rhona, life was all about winning, and she'd beaten the Moo in round one of this contest. Then she thought of Lachlan. One day she would lose.

The girls took her to a long, narrow room that smelt of sweat, urine and sick.

"Miss Blacklock said to bring her," announced Polly. Megan and the other girl must have been at least twelve, but little Polly was clearly the leader. Rhona, with her eyes still closed, couldn't see who the girl was talking to as she got tipped onto a horribly hard bed. She opened one eye a fraction and gave Polly a wink but the younger girl seemed too frightened to wink back and left in a hurry. Not wishing to be dropped in a coffin and taken straight to the morgue, Rhona groaned, opened her eyes wide and stared up at the low ceiling.

She heard a shuffle of footsteps and craned her neck to take in their owner: a white-haired man with long, whiskery sideboards that reached almost to his chin. He wore an ankle-length night-gown that had once been white but was now filthy and stained. There was a mischievous twinkle in eyes so different from the Moo's cruel optical slits that they looked almost friendly.

"You new here, missy?" he asked.

"Aye," replied Rhona. "Fell down the steps to the toilet and..."

"I know! They just don't care. Because we have no families they think – just take them to the sick room and forget about them! Are you all right, lass? No bones broken?"

Rhona sat up.

"I'm fine! I'm a gymnast – see – nothing broken. Oops... shouldn't have said that! You won't tell, will you? Is there another way out of here?"

"Only the way *he's* going!"

The whiskered fellow flicked a thumb at a shrivelled body in the bed next to Rhona's. Its occupant was a man who couldn't have been that old for his hair was still brown, but his skin was as wrinkled as a prune, his eyes sunken and his toothless mouth open. In the bed beyond was a skinny, scared-looking child of about five whose face was covered with red blisters. The other beds lining the long, bare-walled room were filled with similarly-emaciated children. Not one returned Rhona's smile.

"And the rest? They've had no lives, poor darlings – or ever likely to have – so going through the same door that he's approaching will be no great loss for their wee souls."

"I think that's awful!" said Rhona. "They should be in hospital!"

"Without money? What hospital would take them?"

"Where I come from –" the girl began, but then thought the better of trying to explain how in the same city in a different time and another dimension anyone who was ill, however penniless, would get properly looked after. "Never mind! I just have to get out of here!" She slipped her legs over the side of the bed. "Why is that dying man looking at me in a funny way?"

"Probably thinks you're an angel with your pretty face and that dress you're in."

"Someone else said that – but not *him*, worst luck," Rhona added with feeling. "Not the woodcutter's son! He's in love with..."

"*He* was a woodcutter, you know – that bundle of bone wrapped in skin staring at you like you're a vision from heaven. Never be cutting wood again this side of the grave, you mark my words!"

"He's a woodcutter? Wait – does he have a son called Lachlan?" The dying man's eyes widened and fixed on Rhona as his lips began to move soundlessly. He was trying to speak. The girl got down, knelt by his bed and lovingly stroked his mop of brown hair. She asked again: "Do you? Have a son called Lachlan? On the other side of the Wall?"

He nodded.

"Get him some water please!" she instructed the whiskered man. "He's all dried out. You should've thought of that!"

"I'm a patient myself, ken. Only in charge because the nurse was needed to help out in the stone breaking yard. Seems a fight broke out and more than stones were getting broken – then..."

"Hurry! Where's the water?"

"Over there. In that jug." He pointed to a white jug and cup on a stand. Rhona ran to it and picked out a

120

dead fly and other bits of dirt before filling the cup.

"Lift his head!" she ordered on returning with the water. "No! Not like that! Gently!"

Between them, the girl and the patient helped the old woodcutter drink in little sips through parched lips.

"How *could* you let him dry out like this?" scolded Rhona. "Fetch more water!"

After three cupfuls, Lachlan's father managed a smile as the girl carefully rested his head back on the hard bed.

"Don't you have a pillow?" she asked. The white-haired patient looked questioningly down at her. "Yes you do! Tear off the bottom of your nightgown. It's too long anyway. Roll it up. Make a pillow with it."

Rhona helped him rip a sizeable piece of material from his already tattered nightgown. Soon the woodcutter's head was more comfortably supported on the makeshift pillow and Rhona held his hand as she spoke:

"Your son has it. He's the true Keeper of the Sword. Did you know that?" she asked.

The woodcutter nodded.

"He's going to rescue you. He'll be here soon. I was following them..." Rhona saw alarm in the man's eyes at the word 'them'. "Lachlan and my sister, I mean. I'm sure she *is* my sister – but here she's called Mairi."

A solitary tear appeared in the corner the woodcutter's eye. Rhona carefully wiped it with her sleeve.

"The Princess? Little Mairi?" he asked in a barely audible whisper, placing a hand over Rhona's. "Is she grown now? Is she beautiful?" Reluctantly, thinking of her sister together with Lachlan, Rhona agreed she was. "Like her sister then?" queried the woodcutter with a glint in his eye. "I didn't know the Princess had a sister."

"In another place. Look, we've gotta get you to a doctor. Out of this hell hole..."

The woodcutter shook his head.

"No. Let me die. I must die. Before they find out."

"Find out what?"

The woodcutter looked uneasily at the white-whiskered patient who stood in stunned disbelief at the transformation of the dying man.

"He wants you to turn around," Rhona explained to the bewildered man in the torn nightgown. "And cover your ears. So you can't hear what he has to tell me."

Looking like a worn-out ghost, the old patient returned to his bed on the other side of the room. The woodcutter tugged at the girl's arm, pulling her closer.

"Something she found," he whispered. "Hidden in the Princess's bedroom. It's the only way to destroy him."

"The Kelpie? You're talking about the Kelpie?"

The woodcutter nodded.

"She kept it. Later, the King took it to the Seelie Faeries. Just by holding the thing Fiona's grandfather knew. He had a special gift, you see."

"Holding what? Knew what?"

"The only way..." the woodcutter replied. His voice was growing weaker.

"*What?*" the girl insisted.

The woodcutter let go of her hand and pulled the horsehair bedcover up to expose his legs. Rhona gasped when she saw the state of the man's legs, so deformed they were barely recognizable as limbs.

"*They* did that! With one of those big hammers in the stone breaking yard. Trying to get me to tell them. But still I kept quiet. You see, Red Cap killed Fiona's grandfather. Doubt they'll ever forgive him for that. He'll be stuck in that old ruin forever. And the King killed himself with the Sword before the Kelpie could find out. There's just me – and now you. You must never let them know you've spoken with me."

Rhona frowned. She had no idea what the fellow was going on about. Had those awful injuries turned him mad?

"What did Mairi find and what did the faery grandfather discover about it? I have to know!"

"Closer!" the old man urged. Rhona lent forwards and he whispered in her ear.

"A curve made by...?" she began to repeat aloud, frowning, but was silenced by a bony hand placed over her mouth.

"And it must be returned to..." Lachlan's father began to say before he was interrupted by the sound of voices on the other side of the door. "Quick – back to your bed!" he warned.

Rhona ran to her bed and threw herself onto the blanket just as the door opened...

Chapter 12: Fire in the Sick Room

Lachlan cautiously opened the door. Mairi immediately covered her nose, for the smell in the vast hall was awful. High-ceilinged, it was packed with scruffy children standing at long wooden tables and teasing bits of rope with metal spikes. A thin little girl looked up.

"Wow! Another Princess! And that man's got a...!" she began before bringing her small hand up to her mouth.

The stocky woman who had ladled the breakfast porridge in the refectory looked up. Holding a stick, and only yards from Polly, she swivelled and fixed the child with a stare that could have cut through steel. She walked towards her prey like a cat stalking a rabbit, her stick raised. The girl, who'd been unable to stop herself from exclaiming in surprise on seeing Mairi in her fine purple dress and the woodcutter's son carrying a sword, backed away from the woman. The other children stopped working and the eyes of each child showed a mix of relief and fear; relief that *they* were not the foolish one who'd spoken out of place and fear that the next time the woman raised her stick they might be at the receiving end of her anger.

"I'm sorry Miss Moo – I mean – oh dear..."

The woman erupted into a volcano of rage. She shook like an overheated boiler about to burst and her anger must have rendered her blind, for she seemed totally unaware of the beautiful girl in the purple dress and the boy with the Sword. Lachlan was so quick that even if she had seen him she'd not have been able to alter the outcome. Mairi watched in amazement as the boy she used to play with as a little girl leapt forwards; with a dazzling twirl, the blade of his weapon sliced through the Moo's cane as if it were a candy stick. Instead of beating the child, the woman merely swiped the air with a useless stump of a stick clutched in her podgy fist. She turned and emitted a squeaky gasp of alarm on seeing the fiery Sword, its point just inches from her throat.

"Apologise!" the boy demanded. "Say sorry to the child you were about to hit and I may let you live!"

The woman, her ugly face contorted with both fear and fury, glanced at Polly.

"But she – b-b-but I wasn't..." she stammered.

"APOLOGISE!" bellowed Lachlan.

At that point Mairi knew; she knew that her only true friend from the past was also a prince, not a mere peasant boy as her father had called him. *He* was the one who should become King; and the woman the child had referred to as the 'Moo' dropped to her knees and pleaded for mercy.

"Say sorry to the girl and promise me you'll never again hit any of these children!"

"Aye, sir! Forgive me, Polly. I was only doing my job. Doing what they tell me to do."

Mairi went over to Polly and examined the girl's arms. They were covered with bruises.

"We can't leave her here," she said. "She'll have to come with us."

"Only if Megan comes too," insisted Polly. "I'm not leaving her with the Moo without me to protect her."

The face of the woman kneeling before Lachlan grimaced with barely-restrained wrath at the word 'Moo', but she remained still.

"If you ever lay another finger on any of these girls

you'll regret it for the rest of your life... and beyond," warned Lachlan. "And that may come sooner than you think, hen (Scots expression for 'woman')!"

Three girls followed the woodcutter's boy out of the hall.

"I know where she is!" Polly announced once they were outside.

"Who?" asked Mairi.

"The other girl who looks like a princess. Are you related?"

"Rhona? She's here?"

"Aye! We're friends already, ken. Had to take her to the sick room."

"Why?" Mairi looked troubled. "What was Rhona doing in here? And what did that woman do to her?"

"The Moo? She wouldn't dare touch Rhona. No, the other princess fell down the stairs – only didn't actually fall if you get my meaning. It seemed on purpose. Like she was doing a dance down the steps. Quite graceful, really. She knew what she was doing. I could tell. She winked at me when we left her in the sick room. I think she wanted to go there for a reason."

For a brief moment a faraway look came over Mairi as if what the younger child had just said reminded her of something and she was trying hard to remember what it was.

"So you know where the sick room is?" she asked Polly.

"That place? Oh no – I'm not going back there. Might be all right for princesses like you and Rhona and for..." Polly eyed Lachlan with wonder. "And for *him*! But not for the likes of me and Megan."

"He's got the Sword. No one can harm you. We have to find his father. And quickly! Before *they* do."

"The child-catchers? With those big nets?"

"They're here. We saw them."

Polly's eyes widened with fear.

"It's round the corner at the end of the corridor."

With Polly in the lead, and after checking the corridor was empty, they crept on to the sick room.

***

"Rhona!" Mairi exclaimed on opening the door. She ran to the girl stretched out on a bed and hugged her. "Oh Rhona, Rhona! What happened to you? Dancing down the stairs? And how did you end up here in the poorhouse, anyhow?"

Rhona never replied. She didn't get that chance – not after Polly screamed. A dark figure holding a net stood in the doorway right behind Megan. Polly darted forwards to protect her friend as Lachlan ran at the figure. She yanked Megan away from the hideous man whilst another then a third child-catcher entered. Lachlan swished the glowing Sword clean through the skull of the one who'd made for Megan but nothing happened. The cut that should have cleaved the brute in half knitted together with a sizzle. The creature, more spirit than human, laughed when one of its fellows lowered a black net over Polly. Megan reached for her friend and she too got netted.

"Leave them alone!" yelled Mairi. For a brief moment there was silence.

"Oh, we're not interested in these homeless waifs, your Highness. Come quietly – come to your master – and they go free."

Mairi stepped forward a couple of paces then halted.

"First let them go!"

"No, Mairi!" shouted Lachlan. "Don't."

"These girls are my people, Lachlan. I must look after them whatever the price." She addressed the child-catcher: "Take *me* instead. Take me to the Kelpie. Let him have my eyes and my soul. Just leave the girls alone."

"Mairi... NO!" yelled Lachlan.

Slowly, the dark figure raised the net free from the two trembling poorhouse girls who held on to each other whilst Mairi gave herself up to the child-catcher.

"Mairi – please don't!" sobbed Rhona. "You mustn't. You really *are* my sister. I know you are. You can't leave me alone in this place."

"Listen to her!" agreed Lachlan. "We're supposed to have a whole life together."

"The Princess and the woodcutter's son? Oh, how very romantic!" teased the child-catcher. Already, wings were budding from the creature's bony shoulders and his thin pointy nose was curving into a beak.

"Kill me! Now!" implored a wizened man from the bed beyond Rhona's. Lachlan turned and peered at him. He came up closer, leaning forwards in disbelief.

"Father? It – it can't be you!"

"Kill me, son. With the Sword. You must!"

"Stop him!" shrieked a child-snatcher changing into a dark boobrie.

"It's the only way to save her," insisted the woodcutter. "Do it and your power and your love for the Princess will become stronger. It's your only chance."

"But Father...?"

The man waved his hand meaningfully towards Rhona and Lachlan understood. The boy raised the Sword high, point downwards, and, with eyes firmly shut, drove it into the brittle chest of his father. Rhona closed her eyes against the blinding flash. When they opened again, she saw the woodcutter's son standing with his hands around the hilt of the Sword stuck into the bed. The bed was empty. The boy and girl turned together just in time to see Mairi disappear through the doorway, gripped firmly around the waist by a dark boobrie claw. The other two child-catchers, also turning into boobries, barred the way when Lachlan leapt forwards in a futile attempt to save the Princess. But the sneers on their bird-like faces withered when they saw intense gold flames shimmering on the blade of the weapon. One slash and the nearest child-catcher-come-boobrie sizzled as its companion had done earlier, but this was no healing sizzle; the fire from the blade spread rapidly across the creature's body soon reducing it to a heap of smouldering ash. The other boobrie dropped its net and took off along the corridor, but before its wings had grown enough to lift it into the air Lachlan caught its feathered tail with a slicing cut from the Sword. The tail fell and frizzled whilst its owner, still screaming, burned to a frazzle.

But Mairi was gone. Rhona came and stood beside the boy, overcome with guilt for wishing she could take her 'sister's' place as the focus of his affection. She saw the pain in his eyes as he stared at the empty corridor ahead.

"You can't let your father down now," Rhona said quietly. "Save her. Make him proud. Wherever he is, he'll be watching you. I'm sure of it. We girls can tell these things."

Something prevented Rhona from adding 'perhaps I could take her place': the realisation that her love for her 'sister' in that other world was greater than anything imaginable, perhaps matched only by the boy's love for a girl called Mairi. The best thing she could do to please Lachlan would be to help him stop the Kelpie taking the soul of her rival in love.

"Your father told me a secret," she whispered. "Like it was really, really important. About something hidden in the Princess's room in the palace – something she found, he said. Where the curve of...?"

"Shhh!" silenced the boy. "Tell no one else. Not even me. My father trusted you. It's what the Kelpie is so desperate to know and the fewer who know the better. Let's pray Mairi doesn't remember. Until they find out he'll not want to change her – in case that makes her forget."

"But if she's already forgotten he may think there's no point in waiting. In which case we could..." Lachlan looked so worried Rhona halted mid-sentence, regretting what she'd said.

"Whatever, we must get out of here," the boy insisted. "They'll think perhaps my father told you more than he did. The Sword might now be stronger than the dark boobries but it's no match against the Kelpie. Or Auld Clootie. *He'll* know of its weakness, but maybe not its new power. Power that comes from what my father knew. It seems as if the Sword has gained greater strength from my father's spirit."

"How are we going to get to the Wall? You saw all those boobries in the sky. They'll be everywhere."

"Oakum!" suggested Polly. The other three gawped at the wee girl.

"Oakum?" queried Rhona.

"Aye! Oakum. Me and Megan have it planned, don't we, Megan?"

Ever silent, Megan agreed with a nod.

"Explain," urged Lachlan.

"They pack the oakum into big boxes, see? Leave them round the back of the poorhouse to get loaded onto carts. For the shipyards. We could hide in one of those."

"But we have to get to the Wall. To the Necropolis, not the docks," observed Rhona.

"The boy could pull the cart up the hill. If he can kill child-killers he'll easily pull an oakum cart. And we could use that blanket."

She pointed to the blanket on Rhona's bed.

"Allow me to help you, young miss." It was the whiskered patient. In the commotion, Rhona had forgotten all about him. Easing himself to the edge of his bed, he lowered his stick-like legs, now naked to the knees, and, clutching his own blanket, staggered over to Rhona. "Take this too – and I'll get others for the two poorhouse girls. Then hurry. I'll create a diversion. Using this stuff..." He kicked at the glowing embers of the burnt boobrie, sending sparks into the air. Rhona looked puzzled.

"A fire? But what about all the children here?"

"That's just it. They'll come with buckets of water. Desperate to put out the fire. Because anyone of these children might have overheard what you know from the woodcutter."

"Huh! What I *don't* know, you mean. But it's a cool idea."

"Cool? Sounds hot to me," said Lachlan. Rhona blushed crimson.

"Just an expression – where I come from," she replied shyly.

"And leave the door unlocked," added the old patient.

"Unlocked? There'll be no door at all when my Sword's finished with it," promised Lachlan. "And while they're busy putting out the fire we'll quietly slip into the hall and release all the other children. Those child-catchers..."

"Or boobries. The one that survived, that is! Turned back into a boobrie to escape from *you*," interrupted Rhona, brimming with admiration.

"Well – those black things whatever they are. They'll be too busy questioning this lot and looking for you to bother with the bairns in the children's work hall."

After they left the sick room, smoke that curled out into the corridor caused the ill and the dying to cough. Once round the corner, they heard the whiskered man call out:

"FIRE! FIRE!"

They hid in the same cupboard that Lachlan and Mairi had used whilst heavy feet pounded past to deal with the fire. Huddled up against the boy, Rhona sensed Lachlan's anger and upset over his loss: her sister. Earlier she might have been delighted, but now she felt only shame for ever thinking she could take Mairi's place. Whether the red-haired girl was Mairi or Caitlin, Rhona realised was the most important person in the world for her, and prayed they'd get to the Palace in time. How could she ever face her sister if the girl were to become trapped in the spirit of the Kelpie, body and soul? Would Queen Mairi-the-Kelpie even recognise her?

***

Craddick's biggest fear was that he'd be spotted as a gnome covered by a sack and get dragged away to some miserable garden where he might end up amongst tulips and bluebells to be admired by little old ladies in long, flowery dresses. But with all that hurrying and scurrying about of the terrified residents of the City, no one noticed the tatty, squat little figure staring up at the sky. When another dark boobrie flew past, with the Princess held fast by its massive curved dagger claws, he nodded with satisfaction. 'So far, so good,' he thought. He hurried back to the large square where pandemonium was greatest. Standing in the centre of the square he held out his arms and cried out:

"Long live the Kelpie!"

The response was immediate. A boobrie swooped down from a rooftop, its shadow scattering the crowd below until only one little figure was left. The gnome was picked up, as light as a toy for the giant bird, and carried away beyond the square, over the Cathedral, across the Wall, a wall invisible to City folk, towards the Palace. Pleased with what he'd achieved, Craddick set about planning the next stage of his strategy – and his smile left him. Too soon and all would be lost; too late and there'd be nothing to lose.

***

As soon as it had gone quiet in the corridor, Lachlan opened the door. The Sword glimmered faintly enough for the four to see their way to the children's hall. Two blows with the Sword were sufficient to cut slice through the door. In no time, a horde of excited children burst free from the hall, ran down the corridor and gathered before the door to the outside world. A few strikes from the Sword ensured that particular door would never again be used to hold a child inside the poorhouse against its will.

Polly's prediction proved correct. A cart, half-full

133

of oakum, stood unguarded beyond the shattered door. Although the sky was clear and now bird-free, the girls covered themselves with blankets and oakum after climbing in. Rhona feared Lachlan would never be able to push the weight of three girls, even if one *was* little. When the cart jerked forwards, she grinned to herself. He truly was a prince, though sadly her sister's, not her own. What Rhona didn't know was that Lachlan wasn't the only one pushing. A sinewy man called Jamie, who'd returned out of remorse and who felt for the children swarming from the poorhouse, offered to help the boy with the Sword. After a brief exchange of nods and smiles, they bumped the girls hidden in the cart over the cobbles towards the Cathedral.

Rhona's mind filled with the image of the dying woodcutter. How awful it must have been for Lachlan to have to kill his own father, but perhaps he knew more about the magic of the Sword than he let on. Had the man been 'released' rather than 'killed' by the Sword when his useless body vanished? And was the secret she must keep from Lachlan the only thing that could save her sister from an eternity of torment – to be trapped forever as herself, but not truly herself, by the Kelpie.

No one paid heed to the oakum cart being pushed by a man and a boy through the streets of the City. Even after everyone had stopped running around in confusion, folk were huddled in groups talking about the giant black birds as if nothing else mattered. The cart was left at the foot of the Necropolis hill and the girls followed Lachlan and Jamie (Rhona was only mildly disappointed when she discovered it hadn't been Lachlan alone pushing the heavy cart) up the path towards a particular angel tomb. Passing through a wide fissure in the stone, they reached the Wall. Rhona held up the map, Lachlan extended the Sword and they soon found the correct spot. A gap opened, closing behind them.

The Palace, white against the cloudless sky, seemed unreachably high on its craggy cliff. Clusters of huge dark shapes – sentinel boobries – covered the turretswhilst somewhere inside the Palace was Mairi – *loveable* Mairi. Two Rhonas debated with each other: one wanted to run on ahead and demand from whomsoever she found in the Palace to return her sister, but the other Rhona was canny. Either they'd kill her if they knew the secret already or they'd torture her, as they had Lachlan's father. She didn't feel brave enough to get tortured, so she followed Lachlan and Jamie whilst they talked man's stuff, followed herself by Polly and Megan who jabbered young girls' talk. Rhona felt almost alone as they scaled the wooded hill unseen by the dark boobries' sharp eyes before taking the path that wound down past the waterfall towards the blue and yellow plain. She was thankful the Kelpie wasn't lurking in the spray of the fall, but her relief soon transformed into fear – fear that the Kelpie and that evil little Humming Bird had already done the deed. Caitlin, taken over by Mairi, might already be a kelpie in disguise.

Lachlan and Jamie decided it would be suicide to attempt to enter the Palace by daylight. Better pray that Mairi was still Mairi, cross the plain at night and seek help from the Seelie Faeries. They still had the Sword; the secret, assuming Mairi had no recollection of this, remained known to just one living person: *her* – though Rhona failed to see how the woodcutter's dying words could save her sister.

They found a hidden cove on the cliff overlooking the plain. Whilst they sat bunched together, waiting for the sun to sink below the faery wood stretched like a dark green ribbon across the horizon, Rhona listened to the two men. Each had known her sister in a different way: Lachlan as the little red-haired Princess he'd grown so fond of as a child and for whom he'd gladly give his own life as well as that of his father, and Jamie the baker's assistant who knew Mairi as the feisty girl who'd escaped from the orphanage and who was loved by the street children and forever on the run from the child-catchers. The more she heard them talk about these girls, the more she became convinced they were both Caitlin.

"Never without that book of hers!" explained Jamie. "My aunt told me to look out for her when she went missing from the orphanage and I did. Soon found her hiding in a dark alley surrounded by wee bairns. She 'read' to them from the book by showing pictures and making up stories. You could see they adored her from the way they never took their eyes off the girl. I sneaked her some bread and the first thing she did was to break it up and hand it round to the other bairns. The little ones first. Always put herself last. Every day I'd go looking for her and give her bread or other bits of food I managed to scrounge. My aunt told me she was special. When Mairi said back then that she was really the Princess from one of the stories in her book, I thought it was hunger playing tricks on her mind. Now I ken I was wrong and she was right. She did so much for those bairns – and was horribly upset whenever one got snatched by a child-catcher. They tried to use the children to get to her –

and because of one little urchin they almost succeeded. She was forever on the run. Couldn't trust anyone apart from me. Then she disappeared. I worried they'd caught her. That's when I asked to take deliveries to the poorhouse. No one there had heard of a red-haired girl called Mairi. Didn't see her for years. Then I came across her one day near the Cathedral. Grown so beautiful. She'd made friends with a stray kitten and she even fed bread to the starving animal before feeding herself. Only a true Princess would do that, ay?"

Rhona wiped her eyes with the back of her hand. As the drying tears cooled her skin she felt more determined than ever to get her sister back.

Chapter 13: The Story in the Book

Mairi fought against the claws of the dark boobrie, struggling to prise them open. She'd have preferred to have dropped from the sky and fallen to her death somewhere in the City below than to end up prisoner in her own Palace whilst awaiting the attentions of the dreaded Humming Bird. But the more she tried to free herself the tighter the claws squeezed around her middle till she could barely breathe.

Hanging from the bird, she soared over the Cathedral and the Necropolis. Then, as if she'd slipped through an invisible curtain, the scenery changed. No smoke, no grey streets with grey buildings; instead a beautiful landscape of wooded hills rising to a high cliff upon which stood the white Palace where she'd grown up and once been so very happy. Now the same building filled her with fear. Closing her eyes, she attempted to will the boobrie to turn around and take her back to the poorhouse. Even that would have been a better final destination, but it was no use: the beast circled over the Palace before descending into the courtyard.

The landing was surprisingly gentle. The black creature immediately transformed into a child-catcher who gleefully rubbed his hands after delivering Mairi to a pair of gnome guards. A noise above caused the Princess to look up. Another giant black bird, carrying what appeared to be a sack, spiralled out of the sky, dropping its burden just feet away. It took off again as the sack stood up and dusted itself down before removing a layer of sack-cloth.

"Princess, you've returned at last!" announced Craddick, giving a polite bow.

Mairi looked from Craddick to the guards.

"You too?" she queried. "I thought..."

"*I'll* take her to her room," interrupted Craddick. "The Princess must be made comfortable. She'll need to change. For him! Into something more befitting a Princess about to become Queen. He'll be here any minute now that he knows."

"Knows what?" the girl asked, frowning.

"That you've been safely returned to your rightful home. Thanks to the Keeper of the Eyes – as you, yourself, called me, yourHighness! Remember?"

"You're nothing of the sort. You're just a traitor like the rest of these..." Mairi turned to take in the silent rows of gnome guards standing stiffly behind her. "...these horrid little garden gnomes!"

Craddick's eyes flashed anger.

"Your room!" he repeated sharply. "At least you should remember where *that* is, ay?"

Feeling safer with one gnome than with hundreds, Mairi followed Craddick from the courtyard up the winding staircase to the Royal Suite at the top of the Palace. She felt confused. She'd been sure he was on their side, particularly after that fierce battle with Captain Hokkit.

Her room was so clean Mairi could have eaten a fried egg off the floor without one fleck of dust entering her mouth. She sat on the edge of the four-poster bed and scowled at the gnome.

"Don't you remember now?" he asked. His tone had changed and the anger that had altered his face was gone.

"Remember what, you miserable little flower bed

139

decoration?"

"Don't try my patience, Highness. The secret! It was your father who killed himself, you know. If the White Boobrie hadn't taken you away, you'd already be Queen now. Don't you see? The Kelpie only wants what's yours to belong to you. The Palace and – here, come over to the window."

Mairi joined Craddick at the window. She was sorely tempted to grab hold of his baggy gnome pants and heave him over the sill to fall to a certain death for having played games with her by pretending to be on her side.

"Isn't it beautiful?" he said. "All this will be yours when you're Queen."

The girl could not deny the blue and yellow plain was beautiful, stretching away to the distant green forest and snow-capped mountains beyond. But knowing her father's people were trapped like permanent flowers turned that beauty into something uglier than anything she'd ever imagined possible; uglier even than the mean-faced woman at the orphanage who smelt of cabbages and used to beat her.

"I don't want to be Queen any longer," she replied. "Not here."

"You've no choice. Now tell me the secret!" She turned to face Craddick and he could tell from the look in her eyes. "You really don't know?"

She shook her head.

"Perhaps Father didn't tell me for a reason," she said. "Like he killed himself for a reason."

"You must be starving, Highness. I'll get you some food."

"When will...?" began the Princess.

"The Humming Bird? When the time comes. Just make yourself comfortable for now."

After the gnome had left, Mairi leaned out of the window and scanned the empty sky. Why had the White Boobrie abandoned her? And where were Lachlan and the girl called Rhona?

***

Rhona was thankful for the dark clouds that had gathered during the day, for at night not a single star illuminated them as they hurried across the plain towards the forest. When they arrived, a line of bushes moved forwards to greet them. One of these, after changing into a pretty little green-clothed faery, ran on ahead and hugged Rhona.

"You have it?" Fiona asked. "The secret? And where's the Princess?"

Lachlan turned his face away, ashamed of his moistening eyes. He nodded.

"A curve made with fire that holds life between the air and the earth," replied Rhona, also fighting back the tears. "That's all Lachlan's father said. He was about to tell me more but it was too late. The child-catcher came in to..." The girl paused. She felt muddled.

"Where?"

"That place. The – um – the sick room. And he..."

"Asked to be killed by the Sword? Like the King?"

"Yes – but..."

"You were wonderful, Rhona. But a curve made of fire? Life, air and earth? Where? Did he say where?"

"In the Princess's room in the Palace – I think."

"Right under the Kelpie's very nose?"

Rhona pictured that huge nose with hollow black nostrils sniffing out the answer to the riddle and she couldn't bear the thought of it turning into Caitlin's sweet nose.

"We've no time to lose," announced Fiona. "Lachlan, the White Boobrie is waiting."

Sure enough, once the bushes had become a band of faeries armed with silvery bows and gleaming spears, in a space previously hidden from view stood the White Boobrie, magnificent and indestructible. He cocked his head and his eye warmed the girl's heart. Her love for her sister grew so strong she felt ready to take on anyone or anything, if necessary, to free her. The huge, gentle creature told her through her mind to go and stand beside Lachlan. Blushing crimson, she obeyed. With his vast wings outstretched, he lifted his great body into the air, hovered briefly over the standing youngsters then, with the care of a jeweller picking up the most precious gems in the world, he took delicate hold of Rhona and of Lachlan with his each of his enormous, clawed feet. As they sped across the dark plain, Rhona peered over her shoulder to see a sky shimmering green with flying Seelie Faeries. Three, close behind, had grown large and carried Jamie, Polly and Megan in their arms. Poor Megan looked terrified.

"You'll be all right!" Rhona called out to the girl. "My sister will look after you!"

But as they approached the Palace, confidence abandoned her. Grim and menacing, the high building soared into the blackness of the night like the devil's fist, and on every knuckle of the fist perched dark boobries; menacing, prehistoric vultures from an age before goodness came to the world, they waited for the boy who would dare to challenge the Kelpie for the soul of the Princess. Rhona shivered, and the White

Boobrie felt her fear:

"The Woodcutter's son only wants to save her soul, not keep it," he told her mind. "This will give him more strength than you could ever imagine!"

And the White Boobrie's words seemed to shine a beam of hope across the darkness before a blinding light dazzled her. Lachlan had drawn his Sword.

***

Whatever it was Mairi was supposed to remember from those blissful childhood days in her father's Palace had to be important both for her and for the Kelpie. She racked her brains all day but her mind only came up with brief flashes of long-gone happiness such as playing hide-and-seek in the Palace gardens with her mother, picking flowers, or being swung high by her father and laughing till she felt her sides would split. Back then the gnomes were friendly and tended the gardens, often telling her where she might find the prettiest flowers. But one terrible moment kept coming back to her – the moment her father came into her room, the very same room in which she now sat staring at herself in a spotless mirror, to tell her about her beloved mother.

She recalled fear more than grief; fear that her mother would never again hug her or tuck her up into bed after telling one of those lovely stories about the good people of old and the coming of the Seelie Faeries. Her father had said it was an accident. The Queen's horse stumbled on losing a shoe and threw her. Weeks later, when she found a horse-shoe in a meadow, she hid it at first from her father. It was like her secret connection with her mother, and she would sit on her bed, tears streaming, clutching the metal shoe to her chest and talking to her dead mother as if the shoe might magically bring them back together again. Her father told her the horse had galloped away out of shame and vanished forever for he'd been devoted to his mistress.

But her brain could come up with nothing when Craddick returned, demanding she give up her secret before the Humming Bird learned that she was back in the Palace. He reminded her she was now fifteen and her eyes all but belonged to the Kelpie already.

"I'll make it more pleasant for you if you tell me," he promised, but Mairi grew angry and shouted at him to go away and leave her alone. When he finally left in disgust, she was lying face down across the bed, crying.

He descended the stairs, down, down, down to the dungeons below. Forced to cover his large nose with his oversized hand, for the smell was awful, he felt badly for his father. But it had been his father's idea and the only way they, the gnomes, might one day become lords of what was rightfully theirs. Not even Jadda the jailer knew. No one else was to be trusted, so Craddick ordered the brainless gnome who carried the ring of jail keys to take a break. He, Captain Craddick, wished to question the chief prisoner. When alone, Craddick approached the jail – the one in which Mairi had been held captive. The key made a clunk, the lock snapped free and the door, on being opened, groaned like a sick old man. The torch on the wall had burned out, leaving only a faint glow.

"Father?" he called out.

Ex-Captain Hokkit's wrinkled face appeared in the gloom.

"Took your time, didn't you, son?" he replied crossly.

"She says she doesn't know but I don't believe her. And the Kelpie might return any minute now. Those wretched dark boobries – or even Auld Clootie himself – will have got the boy."

"Our spies found her book in the cave and brought it to me," said the old man. "The book she stole in the City. Was never without it, some say! The Kelpie knows nothing about the book, of course. Don't you think it might give us a clue?"

Craddick took a torch from one of the other cells, leaving a poor prisoner in total darkness. Father and son sat on the narrow bunk flicking through the pages of the tattered book of fairytales. Those telling the story of the Princess and woodcutter's son were so well thumbed they'd turned a dull shade of grey, the smudged words merging with the frayed paper, but the pictures were unmistakable. They showed the Palace with the King exactly as Craddick remembered him, with gnomes tending the gardens; the plain beyond the Palace was green, not yellow and blue, and there were people in the Palace courtyard rather than gnomes.

"Is that how you want it to be again?" asked Hokkit. "Because when he has her eyes and her soul he'll bring the people back. To be *his* subjects. He's been using us all the time! Oh, you've failed me son! The idea was for her to trust you. Think of you as a friend. And even the White Boobrie was helping you, unknown to him. Now all those gnomes died in battle for no good reason other than that I should get the blame and you the glory. Without the secret we'll all end up back in those awful gardens looking after flowers again. An accursed nightmare, son! That's what it's come to!"

"Father, I did try. I even felt for the Princess when she flew past in the claws of a boobrie. I – wait a minute – the book. What if I return the book to her? She's sure to trust me then. And bound to remember on seeing it."

"Meanwhile I rot in this stinking hole!"

"I'll ask the Princess to grant you an amnesty. Make her believe I'm good and kind and therefore to be trusted. All part of my plan, ay?"

"Huh! Does she know I'm your father?"

"No one knows. Only mother – and she's..."

"Yes, yes. Don't remind me. She, too, loved the Queen. She said what she believed in and died for it. It was how the Kelpie made me swear allegiance. Showed me the hammer they'd use if I crossed over to the enemy – which is why *you're* the one pretending to work for the Princess... in case he should suspect. Oh, I just wish it was all over."

"It will be soon, Father. She'll remember with the book. Books are always full of memories. *You* told me that, once. And when we know the secret we'll have power over the Kelpie!"

Clutching the Book of Fairytales, Craddick scaled the spiral staircase to the fifteenth floor. He changed tactic: crouching beside the bed, he carefully placed the book next to the Princess, open at the first picture of *The Princess and the Woodcutter's Son.*

Mairi rolled over and stroked the page with the tips of her fingers. The young man there was the spitting image of Lachlan.

"I can't read," she said quietly.

"That makes two of us then," chuckled the gnome. "Look, sorry I got a bit cross. I just can't bear the thought of you becoming the Kelpie – and being cruel.

I want to help. With the secret we could destroy him together. We might even..."

Craddick couldn't finish the sentence. It was too painful to say what he hoped for.

"How many times do I have to tell you? I do *not* know what the secret is! I've tried to remember all afternoon. When I was standing at the window and looking out at the forest where Lachlan and I used to play, I prayed it would come back to me. Maybe the Seelie Faeries know – if the secret is still out there somewhere. They know everything about the forest."

"Princess – this book – apparently you always kept it with you in the City. Doesn't it tell you anything?"

"Only that..." Mairi touched the face of the boy in the picture. "Never mind. And who are you really working for? Tell me! Auld Clootie?"

"Oh mistress – how could you? For yourself, Highness! As you are – and *will* be when Queen."

Almost true, only would Queen Mairi, the gnome wondered, be like her father, forcing gnomes to tend the royal gardens again? He had to make a difficult decision.

"Go away!" Mairi snapped. "I don't believe you – and I don't want you anywhere near me when it happens."

"Please, read this."

"I can't read! Wait a minute – those words! They're telling me things – as if speaking to me." She sat up abruptly, holding the book. "I can – no it's not true – can't be – but yes! I *can* read! Leave me alone! I want to read. Read my story. *Our* story!"

Craddick left with a mix of excitement and sadness in his heart for he knew 'our' could never involve him.

Later, when it had grown dark outside, and when

Mairi had read not only *The Princess and the Woodcutter's Son* but also half the other stories, she closed the book and, smiling, she hugged it as she might a long lost friend. She drifted off to sleep, thinking of Lachlan, and awoke still thinking of the boy, still smiling. But the smile vanished when a horribly familiar sound from the other side of the door needled into her brain. Frantically, she tried to think of somewhere to hide the book. The door creaked open as she quickly reached down to slip the book underneath her bed.

Chapter 14: Forgotten Secret

The Humming Bird drifted into the Princess's chamber.

When the little silver creature hovered above Mairi, she remained still as if held fast by an invisible cobweb. The mere sound of its hum instilled obedience in the girl. She was about to own up to the book being secreted under the bed, but an image in her mind of her and the woodcutter's son holding hands gave her just enough strength to remain silent. When the Kelpie entered, even that vestige of strength vanished.

"My Lord, I put the b–," she began her confession.

"Quiet, Princess! First tell me all that you know. We don't have much time. But as Queen you'll have all eternity as you and me together. Just think of that. And think about the power you'll have. So tell me what you know of the secret."

Mairi was about to blurt out something that occurred to her whilst reading the *Princess and the Woodcutter's Son* – something to do with her mother – when a blinding flash lit up the room, casting a huge horse shadow across one wall. The Humming Bird fluttered back towards the safety of its Master. The demon horse whinnied and reared up, confused and disturbed. At the same time, horse and Humming Bird were joined by the diminutive figure of a gnome: Craddick had returned, bearing a sword. He went to the window and opened it, only to be bowled onto his back by the thrust of a great white claw. Someone else now stood beside the floored gnome. Mairi stared at the silhouetted figure of a girl.

"Rhona – is it you?" she asked.

Before the girl could answer another white claw and another body appeared, and a new whiteness was within the chamber, streaming from the Sword held by the boy. Moments later three Seelie Faeries sailed into the room, depositing two surprised-looking Victorian pauper girls and an out-of-place Victorian baker's assistant. All three blinked a few times before deciding whether they were dreaming or awake.

"Leave!" Lachlan commanded of the Kelpie. "You don't belong to this world. Neither does that venomous little bird of yours. Leave before I slice you into horse meat!"

"You? A woodcutter's son? Challenging the great Kelpie? Come on then, little boy – show me what you can do!"

With a single swish of his Sword, Lachlan cut clean through the beast's thick neck. Nothing happened. He pushed the point of the weapon almost to the hilt into one of those hollow eye sockets, but the beast only laughed. Starting to panic, the woodcutter's son focused on the Humming Bird, slashing and hacking at the air but the bird was always a split second ahead of him. Those years of practice seemed fruitless: the Kelpie and his evil avian partner were invincible.

But Lachlan was not one to give up. He glanced at his terrified friend from the past as she looked from the Kelpie to himself, uncertain who she really wanted to win this contest of strength. It was only after Rhona ran to the Princess and threw her arms about her sister that the older girl seemed to snap out of a trance.

"LACHLAN!" Mairi screamed.

Lachlan turned, and in that moment of distraction

Craddick's big hand reached up from the floor and snatched the Sword from the boy. The gnome stood up, waving the weapon threateningly, forcing the woodcutter's son to step back against the open window.

"Didn't I always say I was both Keeper of the Sword *and* the Eyes, Master?" he announced. "So, miserable peasant boy, what's it to be? Death as a hero at the point of the Sword you tried to steal from me or death as a coward – a fifteen storey drop to the ground below?"

But when he stabbed at Lachlan two things happened: first, the Sword that no longer glowed in the gnome's gnarled hand seemed to stick every time the tiresome little traitor lunged at the boy; second, in a burst of growls, a group of gnome guards entered the Royal Chamber. They ran, grunting and shrieking towards Rhona and her friends with raised weapons but got no further than half way across the chamber. The three Seelie Faeries lifted themselves into the air and, floating above the gnomes, held them fast as if their pointy boots had turned to glue. Motionless as their garden cousins, they could only grumble and squeak. Still wary of the Sword, the woodcutter's son edged towards Craddick and the gnome captain backed away. Victory seemed within the boy's grasp until the Kelpie intervened. Rising up on his hind legs, he towered over Lachlan, trapping him like a bound prisoner. Water dripped onto the boy from the beast's silvery hooves as he spoke:

"I've had enough of this entertainment! The time has come, Princess. If you want the boy to live and remain as your servant chopping wood for the Palace, open your eyes for the Humming Bird. Allow our souls to merge and I shall have your body as well. You and I shall reign together forever. The City will be ours too. And all other lands joined to us by rock or by water."

Mairi rose from the bed and walked slowly towards the Humming Bird with a determination Rhona had never before seen in her sister. *She* had always been the strong-minded one, determined to win every sporting competition she entered. Yet here was a fight she had already lost; a fight to save Caitlin from eternal damnation as the evil Queen Mairi, a living human shell for Auld Clootie's Kelpie.

"Your shoes, Princess!" ordered the Kelpie. "By your bed! The shoes of gold that only the Queen may wear. Put them on. After the Humming Bird has done his work, you and I will go out onto the Royal balcony as one. You'll call out to your people. And some, the chosen few, will arise from the plain and enter the Palace as your subjects. As for the others – well, my new eyes will want something to look out over every morning when we arise, ay? All those pretty flowers? So, your Highness, your shoes – please."

"Wait a minute!" exclaimed Craddick. "You're bringing the people back into the Palace? But what about us gnomes? What about me? And... and...?"

"And your father? You thought I didn't know? Let's just say you'll keep the gardens tidy for your Queen or get smashed into chippings for the paths."

The whine of the Humming Bird was driving Rhona to distraction as she frantically scanned the Royal Chamber for a clue to the riddle of the secret. The Princess obediently returned to her bed to retrieve the Royal footwear and the bird came closer, its long, thin, worm-like tongue flicking in greedy anticipation of sucking out the girl's soul through her eyes. The teasing whine of the bird's transparent wings seemed to challenge Rhona and she'd never been one to refuse a challenge.

Mairi had difficulty slipping into the golden shoes.

"These shoes, Master," she began. "They're too..."

She didn't get to finish her sentence; a shrill scream pierced the still air like a dart. As the Humming Bird was drifting past the gnome captain, its slim, curved beak directed at the eyes of the Princess, Craddick snatched it from the air with his huge hand. He held it fast at arm's length, its whining wings silenced by his strong fist. It squealed like a piglet being throttled and stabbed at the gnome's fingers with the point of its beak, but Craddick was in no mood to let go.

"My shoes, Master..." repeated Mairi. "They're too small."

"Master? He's only a stupid horse!" grunted Craddick.

Horse... shoes... a curve... a curve made by fire... a blacksmith's fire... life, air and earth... a horse-shoe! Rhona's blue eyes sparkled like sapphires but no one noticed.

"Stop the gnome!" bellowed the Kelpie. "If you don't call him off, Princess, I'll crush the boy into bone dust!"

So concerned was the Kelpie that no further harm should come to his Humming Bird, now limp in the gnome's grasp, he failed to sense Rhona move sideways little by little. With her back to the wall, she felt for something that had been staring at her since the White Boobrie brought her and Lachlan to the Royal Chamber. Her fingers now touched it and traced its curve. Unobserved by the sightless beast poised ready to kill the boy, she took the rusty old horse-shoe off the wall. Although it felt coarse and worthless, she knew this was the most valuable thing she would ever hold.

She gripped the horse-shoe as she had once held a discus. As always, she'd won that particular event hands down, but here was one contest she could not afford to lose. Rhona knew she was right about the riddle for it suddenly made sense: a simple horseshoe, made in the fire of a blacksmith's furnace, that would turn the Kelpie from Auld Clootie's beast back into a Palace horse: the one that had caused the death of Mairi's mother all those years ago after the shoe fell off, making the animal stumble.

Without attracting attention, Rhona brought her arm round, took aim, and swung the horse-shoe in an arc. As it left her hand, the Kelpie, distracted, turned. Knowing he could only feel rather than see when something was amiss, she watched as the horse-shoe hit the puzzled beast's raised silver hoof with the precision expected from a true sportswoman. The horse whinnied. Its silvery sheen turned brown, starting with the hoof and quickly spreading all over the animal from front to back. Lachlan, as if emerging from a dream, pulled himself forwards just before the horse clomped to the floor. Rhona ran to her sister and held her lovingly.

"Rhona? Is it really you? And am I still me? What happened? When that little bird came up close my whole life seemed to drain from me – like my soul was full of holes and..."

"You're gonna be fine, sis!" reassured the younger girl.

"But what about...?" Mairi peered anxiously over

Rhona's shoulder at the woodcutter's son sprawled out on the floor. The crumpled Humming Bird lay beside him. Craddick, holding the Sword, stood over the boy. Rhona saw pain in the other girl's eyes as tears welled.

"Here, Lachlan! It's yours," said Craddick, offering the boy the Sword. In Lachlan's hand the Sword once again shone with white fire. "Princess, please forgive me. The Kelpie got me all confused," explained the gnome. "Your beauty too. I think I hoped – but no, the boy is the Keeper of the Sword. *He* is your true Prince."

Lachlan rose up to look down at the gnome.

"Tell that to your fellow warriors, Captain. Tell them I offer amnesty to all who support the Princess. I'm sure she'll not want ornamental gnomes in her garden when Queen. Right, Mairi?"

Mairi laughed. Rhona was over the moon to see her sister happy again. The Seelie Faeries moved away from the frozen gnome soldiers, allowing them to kneel in homage before the Princess.

"Long live Queen Mairi!" growled Craddick.

"Long live the Queen!" echoed his soldiers.

"Your Majesty, I fear you're still in danger," said Craddick. "See – the Sword burns with a fierce fire."

Shouts from the courtyard outside startled Rhona. She ran to the window.

"Heaven forbid! Lachlan – look!"

The boy joined her. Down below, huge black birds were attacking gnome guards, pecking them with vicious beaks, tearing and ripping with talons of death. Several had morphed into child-catchers in black garments who swung spiked black clubs that set tubby gnomes spinning like tops. Darting Seelie Faeries fired silver arrows with pin-point precision and dived at the

155

boobries with their silver spears but the fearsome birds kept on coming in ceaseless black waves.

"Stay here," Lachlan told Rhona. "Look after the Princess – I meanQueen."

The younger girl hesitated, pulled between staying at her sister's side and impressing her hero in the battle below.

"*I* can fight," announced Polly. "Been doing it all my life!"

"Me too," agreed Megan.

"No!" insisted Jamie. "*All* you girls have suffered enough. Stay and help Mairi. You might become ladies-in-waiting for our new Queen."

"Oooh! Can we really?" asked Megan. "*Real* ladies?"

"Only as friends and equals!" insisted Mairi.

"Can you do anything with this horse?" Jamie asked Lachlan. "Seems to have lost the power of speech but I think he's trying to tell you something."

The horse bowed its head at the boy. When it looked up Jamie and Lachlan gasped. Its eyes had been gouged out. So the Kelpie too had been a victim of Auld Clootie. Lachlan raised the glowing Sword and gently touched each eye socket. The eyes of the horse returned; although the creature could no longer speak, the eyes were saying 'thank you'.

"I remember!" exclaimed Mairi. They turned to look at her. "The day my mother died. I was crying when I got up that morning. Father came into this very room to comfort me. He said not to be sad and that Mother would play with me when she got back from riding. She always went out early. She told me once how she loved the freshness of dawn. You see, I didn't want her to go riding that day but it was too late.

Father promised she'd be fine because she was the best horsewoman in the Kingdom – but I knew something was going to happen. It was that new stable-man. I could feel the evil in his eyes. I thought..." Mairi stopped and wiped away the tears. "I *know* now he was Auld Clootie himself."

"Of course!" exclaimed the woodcutter's son. He jumped up onto the horse, bareback, and kicked its flanks. The girls watched open-mouthed as the horse galloped at the open window, leapt over the sill and was gone. Mairi screamed and ran to the window; down in the courtyard below, her friend from the past was hacking and cutting at black shapes that, one by one, vanished before the shining blade of the Sword. But more and more dark boobries swooped from the sky. Jamie hurriedly led the gnomes out of the chamber and down the winding staircase to join the fray. Rhona, Mairi and the girls from the poorhouse stared from the window, helpless, but no force of evil seemed able to stand up against the power of the boy-turned-Prince on his magnificent horse. Soon just one black figure remained. Unlike the other child-catchers, its hood was hollow and it wielded not a club but a long, curved scythe. The horse bucked and stamped when Lachlan urged it to charge at the figure.

"Auld Clootie!" whispered Polly.

She and Megan hid their faces, but the two sisters stared in horror as the woodcutter's son dismounted and approached the figure, his Sword raised. The Devil swung his scythe at Lachlan, but the boy was quick. He leapt over the silver blade and backed away as the faceless figure glided forwards. Again the scythe cut through the air and again the boy jumped just in time. He slashed at theDevil's arm but his Sword made no impression. To Rhona, all seemed lost. The Devil was playing with Lachlan, making the boy jump with every swish of the Scythe, forcing him back against the wall. Tears streamed down the girl's cheeks whilst Mairi just stood and watched. Had the Kelpie taken her sister's soul already and delivered it to Auld Clootie? Rhona was about to leap from the window as she'd once leapt from the tower to save Mairi from the Humming Bird, when suddenly Mairi leaned out and called down to Lachlan:

"Remember our promise to each other as children! That we'll always stay together whatever happens! Not even Auld Clootie can keep us apart!"

The words had an extraordinary effect on the horse. He shot forwards, jumped over the black-cloaked figure and landed beside Lachlan. The boy scrambled onto the beast's back and together they circled round Auld Clootie, now this way, now that. The Devil faltered, not knowing which way to swing his scythe. *He* had become part of Lachlan's game.

"I love you," called the Princess – the very words that had also formed inside Rhona's head.

One more turn and the empty black hood was looking straight up at the woodcutter's son. Lachlan seized his chance. Holding the Sword point down, he drove it into that dark space. Like lightning in reverse, a blinding flash zigzagged from the black figure into the sky, accompanied by a terrifying scream. Rhona covered her ears and closed her eyes. When opened again, they revealed a very different picture: Lachlan sat proudly on the brown horse. Lachlan the King. There was no Sword, no scythe and Auld Clootie was gone.

The three Seelie Faeries joined the girls at the

window.

"We always knew," said Fiona. "That Lachlan had to be King! Look! Up in the sky!"

The girls looked up and saw the White Boobrie circle high above the Palace. Each knew, in her own way, that the magical bird had changed her story forever. None could say the evil would never return, for Auld Clootie is indestructible, but for now he and his minions, the dark boobries and the child-catchers, were no longer a threat. Mairi was Queen as herself and would bring back her people from their torment. When King Lachlan looked up at his Queen, Rhona knew her time had come to say goodbye forever to her dear sister. She hugged the other girl, but looked away as they parted. Not because of the tears but because she feared that if she looked into her sister's eyes now she'd never pull herself free – like those yellow and blue flowers turning back into living souls, she would stay for all eternity in this extraordinary land. She knew what she had to do. The White Boobrie was telling her. After climbing up onto the sill she leapt from the window. For a brief moment she prayed the handsome woodcutter's son would spread wide his arms and catch her, but he had eyes only for his Queen. Rhona was no longer a part of his story and had in all probability become invisible to him.

The White Boobrie gently caught her and carried her high above the clouds across the lush green plain towards the Forest of the Seelie Faeries. Behind her, a swarm of green faeries flew in formation and they crowded around the girl after they landed in the Faerie Glen. Before flying off, the White Boobie spoke inside her head:

"Thank you, Rhona. I always knew that only you

could save your sister from an evil worse than anything I ever imagined possible. You'll always be one of Life's winners. Never forget that."

As Fiona led Rhona to the faery house, the girl realised she would soon return to another land to be among those she loved, but was sad to be leaving behind others she also loved. As before, inside the faery house she was confronted by a limitless space the size of the Universe, but there in a corner was her familiar bed; this time, only one bed. She snuggled down under the green covers and drifted off to sleep.

***

"Are you all right?" asked a familiar voice.

Rhona opened her eyes. Her father peered down at her. Rhona sat up and rubbed the back of her head. It was sore where she'd banged it on a rock after slipping down to the burn below.

"Think so, Dad," she said.

"You've been out for the count. I was afraid..."

"Where's Caitlin?" Rhona interrupted. "Tell me she'll be okay." Her father merely looked up at the cliff-top above where the blades of a helicopter whirred like a million humming birds rolled into one. "You found her?"

Her father shook his head.

"No, *you* did!"

"And... and she's all right, isn't she? Please say Caitlin's going to be okay."

Her father paused before replying:

"They're doing what they can, Rhona. You were very brave trying to rescue her. I'm so proud of you. You always have been a winner. Never forget that."

Rhona knew from her father's expression that all was *not* right. She scanned the sky, hoping to see a great white bird, but the sky was filled only with grey clouds and tears from heaven that wetted her face.

"She's not...?" Rhona couldn't say the word. It seemed too terrible, and to say the word now would be giving in to death. Both the White Boobrie and her father had told her never to forget she was one of Life's winners. She'd fight for Caitlin. *She* wouldn't let her sister die.

"Dad, I must be with her," she insisted.

"Not even I or your mum are allowed in the helicopter whilst they're – whilst they do what they can. She'd been in the water too long, Rhona. They'll take her to hospital any minute now."

"Dad – you've *got* to make them let me be with her. It might be her only chance."

When it became clear that Rhona would not take 'no' for an answer she was allowed into the helicopter to sit beside her sister whilst paramedics did things to Caitlin with tubes and masks and machines. When they arrived at the Borders General Hospital in Melrose, the doctors told Rhona and her parents it was nothing short of a miracle that the older girl was still alive, but they could make no promises: she was still, as they put it, 'critical'.

Chapter 15: The Return of the Princess

Caitlin opened her eyes and blinked a few times. The whiteness remained, as did that thing covering her mouth and nose. She reached up with her hand.

"Ouch"!" she cried out as something nipped at her arm.

"Caitlin?" a voice said.

Yes, I'm Caitlin. Not Mairi. But why is everything so white? The Great Whiteness?

Then she remembered.

"My eyes... my soul!" she screamed.

"There, there, sis!" said a calming voice she knew so well.

"Rhona? Is that you?"

"You're gonna be fine, the doctor says."

Caitlin eased her head round. She'd never before felt so relieved as at that very moment when her younger sister's smile came into focus. Behind Rhona stood a woman dressed like a nurse. She, too, had a lovely smile.

"I can see! He didn't steal my eyes after all. Or my... ouch! What's that pricking my arm? That tube thing. And what am I doing here?"

"You're in the Borders General Hospital. You fell at the Grey Mare's Tail. It was touch and go in the helicopter but you're gonna be okay."

"Where are Mum and Dad?"

"Oh, it's been hard for them. And Dad blames himself. For saying 'she's such a bookworm – we must take her out today on her birthday come rain or shine!' It started raining when we got there – and, well the

162

grass was all slippery. Please tell him it wasn't his fault."

Caitlin propped herself up on her elbow and pulled the face-mask away from her mouth and nose.

"Of course it wasn't Dad's fault! I love him too much for it to be his fault. It was the Kelpie's!"

Rhona gaped at her sister in shock.

"So – it was true then?" she asked. "It *was* you after all!"

And that's when Caitlin knew there was one thing she had yet to do. As soon as she got back home she went straight to her room to look for something: the book she'd begun the morning she turned fifteen. It was there on her bedside cabinet where she had angrily slammed it down when her father called out that it was time to leave. *Why do I have to go on a birthday picnic when I've an unfinished book to read?* she recalled thinking. *A lovely day for a walk?* Famous last words! The heavens opened on top of them as they struggled up the steep slope beside the Grey Mare's Tail. *'Not forecast,'* her Dad had grumbled! *'What is?'* Caitlin remembered asking grumpily as she pulled her sopping wet jumper around her whilst wondering: *and what's real and what's more than real? That book is definitely more than real.*

Caitlin took her laptop down from the shelf and turned it on. She opened up a blank 'Word' page and looked only briefly at the wordless whiteness – the scary Great Whiteness in which anything could happen! All that day and the next she typed away, thankful for a few days' respite before she would be well enough to return to school. She typed so fast, so accurately, that after a while she didn't even bother to stop and check for errors. Not even Rhona knew what she was up to. Forever the sporty sibling, Rhona spent her time recuperating by practising gymnastics or going for bike-rides, but she guessed Caitlin was up to something, such was the understanding between them.

Left alone to rewrite the book, once again Caitlin became Mairi and the orphan girl's story was retold. This time the truth came out: all along the child had been the heir to the throne and her friend, the woodcutter's boy, would one day reign by her side. She picked up the book to find out who the publisher was. For some reason her eyes kept being drawn to the name – E. K. Pile Ltd – till it dawned on her: Kelpie! She threw the book in the bin, took one of her favourite books from the bookcase, Googled its publisher and e-mailed 'The Return of the Princess' to the e-address given.

The following Monday, school was as it had always been. The sisters' accident at the Grey Mare's Tail had been all over the news, so naturally the day began with them being bombarded with questions in the playground. That didn't last long, and before the morning bell went Rhona was alone, searching her schoolbag for material for the first lesson. Something caught her eye. She looked up and stared in shock. A few yards away stood a new boy, also by himself – a new boy she knew so well. Their eyes met and he smiled. He walked over to her. She opened her mouth and tried to speak, but no words came out. She wasn't good with words – not like Caitlin.

"Hello," he said. Even the voice was the same.

"Yes," she said nervously. "Um – hello. Have you – I mean – what...?"

He held a finger to his lips and she nodded.

"Does Caitlin know?" she asked. He shook his head. "She'll be so excited," the girl added. "She's over there – with her friends. You *will* be in her class, won't you? Same birthday?"

"Aye – and my brother will be in yours! The spitting image of me! Can't miss him."

"Brother? You never said!"

"You never asked!" he answered and winked.

The bell rang. As they bustled into the school building, Rhona felt happier than ever before. Like her sister, she too wondered what was real and what was a story come true; a story *more* than real.

The Author

Oliver Eade, born a Londoner and now an adopted Scot, retired from a career in hospital medicine thinking 'feet up and watch the telly', but this wasn't to be. After waking up one night with a ghost story in his head, he took to writing adult short stories. Over fifty have been published, several winning prizes, and some appear in a collection, **Lost Whispers**. His first young readers' book, **Moon Rabbit**, a magical journey to Mythological China (Oliver's wife is Chinese), was published in 2009. It was a winner of the Writers' and Artists' 2007 New Novel Competition and long-listed for the Waterstone's Children's Book Prize, 2008. The sequel, **Monkey King's Revenge**, came out in 2011 and was a children's genre finalist for the 2012 **People's Book Prize**. **Northwards**, a young readers' dark fantasy based in Texas and the Arctic, was published in 2010. **The Rainbow Animal**, a fun spoof on war, is also set in North America where Oliver's two eldest granddaughters live.

His debut adult novel, **A Single Petal**, which won the Local Legend 2012 Spiritual Writing Competition, is set in Tang Dynasty China (Local Legend Press).

The Terminus, Oliver's debut young adult novel, returns to the city in which he was brought up; a city now changed beyond recognition from the drab post-Word War II era and which, in a post-apocalyptic world, gives Mankind a second chance.

Although not confined to any particular genre, Oliver feels most comfortable in that magical space between reality and fantasy; the space into and out of which children slip so easily in their play; the place of dreams and myths and legends and deeply ingrained in many cultures across the globe.

Website:
www.olivereade.co.uk

Blogs:
http://olivereade.blogspot.co.uk/
http://runawaywheeliebin.blogspot.co.uk/
http://childrenaswriters.blogspot.co.uk/

I'd love to hear from you!
Contact: olivereade@googlemail.com

Novels by Oliver Eade also as e-books:

For young readers:
Moon Rabbit: Stevie Scott from Peebles, Scotland befriends Maisie Wu, a new girl from China, when she when she gets teased for being different. Early one morning he takes her to the river to see the ducklings, she falls, can't swim and he dives in to rescue her. They emerge in mythological China, but have to undertake a perilous mission before they can get back Peebles. A fun introduction to mythical Chinese beasts

and legends.

Monkey King's Revenge: Sequel to *Moon Rabbit* (available as print book only).

Northwards: Strong-minded Texan schoolgirl, Jenny Macnamara, is sent by Earth Mother on a journey to the high Arctic to save the world from a terrifying evil force.

The Rainbow Animal: Rachel takes her pet hamster on a birthday ride on strange-looking animal on a local mall carousel only to end up embroiled in a paint war between the Colorwallies and Dullabillies.

For adults:

A Single Petal: A widowed village teacher in Tang Dynasty China links the death of his merchant friend with the disappearance of local Miao girls, endangering himself and his daughter as he digs more deeply into the mystery.

Lost Whispers: A collection of short stories inspired by travels across the globe.

Plays:

The Gap: Staged in Scotland 2012, a one act surreal comedy about a dysfunctional Peacehaven family split apart when the earth divides into two along the Greenwich Meridian.

Other **Mauve Square** books for young readers:

The Rainbow Animal by Oliver Eade. '... *The Rainbow Animal is an entertaining and thoughtful story about the futility of war and the similarities between people as Rachel and Alec try to prevent the paint war which threatens to destroy the peaceful* *lives of two communities.'*

Ninja Nan and Sidekick Grandad, Ninja Nan Strikes Again, Ninja Nan and the Trio of Trouble. Ninja Man and her Merry Men by Annaliese Matheron. *'...Such an imagination from the author – read these books to your children or grandchildren or even someone else's children and you get to enjoy them again and again!'*

Wolflore by Annaliese Matheron *'...This is a gripping story, multi-layered, beautifully written, but above all else full of humanity... despite being about Werewolves!'*

The Ghost Within by Charlotte Bloomfield. *'This book is a fantastic read, my 12 year old daughter and I thoroughly enjoyed reading it and couldn't put it down. Great story and characters. Much recommended fab little book!'*

Corridor of Doors by Charlotte Bloomfield. 'This is a fab book for children and adults. The style of writing is so imaginative that you really do get drawn into the story and you really can visualise the characters and eerie settings!'

The Shadow of Atlantis, The Shadow of the Pyramid, The Shadow of the Volcano, The Shadow of the Minotaur, The Shadow of the Trojan Horse, The Shadow of Camelot by Wendy Leighton-Porter. *'...Wendy has written a fantastic series of books (Shadows from the Past) filled with mystery, suspense, and adventure.'*

Acknowledgements

I am indebted to my friend, David Jones, for his helpful comments and advice, and to Mauve Square Publishing for editorial and proofreading input. I am grateful to my granddaughters whose sisterly love inspired the story and, above all else, my beloved wife Yvonne Wei-Lun for her seemingly limitless tolerance and understanding. It was bad enough for her to be married to a doctor all those years of interrupted nights and medical moods and frowns, but to have this item replaced by a perpetually anguished writer would, for many, have been the last straw. I also wish to thank writing colleagues, including those in the Borders Writers Forum and The Society of Medical Writers, for their gracious support.

Lightning Source UK Ltd.
Milton Keynes UK
UKOW05f0830260614

234083UK00001B/62/P